THE SCOTTISH FICTION REPRINT LIBRARY

POOR TOM

by

EDWIN MUIR

Introduction by
Professor P. H. Butter

Paul Harris Publishing Edinburgh

M 150914

First Published by J. M. Dent & Sons Ltd, London 1932

This edition first published 1982 in Great Britain by
PAUL HARRIS PUBLISHING
40 York Place
Edinburgh

Introduction by P. H. Butter

ISBN 0 86228 023 0

The publishers acknowledge the financial assistance of the Scottish Arts Council
in the publication of this volume.

Printed in Great Britain by A. Wheaton & Co Ltd, Exeter

INTRODUCTION

WHEN sending POOR TOM to his sister Elizabeth, Muir warned her not to 'look for any living model (or dead one either) for any of the characters'. Nevertheless it is clearly based upon his early years in Glasgow, as he implicitly acknowledged by repeating, in substance or even exactly, several passages from it in his AUTOBIOGRAPHY. During that time (1902-7), as a boy of fourteen to nineteen, he was 'merely stunned' by the successive deaths in his family - of his father, two brothers and mother. 'I was too young for so much death'. Some of the feelings suppressed in those years came out later in dreams. In a dream connected with his mother he 'wept for her the tears I could not weep at her death, when life seemed to be ruled by an iron law, the only response to which was a stupefied calm'. Another way to release and see meaning in suppressed experience was to transmute it into art, as he tried to do in two at least of his three novels. His first novel THE MARIONETTE (1927) is the furthest removed from his own experience, and is probably his best. The next, THE THREE BROTHERS (1931), approaches closer, dealing with the relationship of brothers and with a death in some ways like that of his brother Willie, though in it he tries to achieve distance by setting the action in sixteenth-century Edinburgh. In POOR TOM (1932) he bravely moves closer still, describing a death very like that of his brother Johnnie, set in the Glasgow he had known - bravely because of the difficulty of handling such sensitive material with the detachment he knew was needed in art.

He tries to achieve the necessary detachment by introducing purely imaginary elements, especially the connection of Tom's accident with the love affairs of the two brothers; by bringing together aspects of his own experience from different times, so quite successfully forming a concentrated fictional, rather than an autobiographical structure; and by differentiating the central character, Mansie Manson, the only one to be seen from the inside, from himself. Enough distance might have been attained simply by differentiating the narrator, the mature Muir, from the character as his younger self; and this is what in effect happens for much of the time. But, initially at least, Muir seems to want to go further, to create a quite distinct character for Mansie. As at first presented, Mansie is a conventional young man, popular, successful at work, rather self-satisfied and priggish, not a great reader; he is made to speak, and at times to think, in clichés; and is said to be a person without 'any great intelligence or sincerity of mind' (233). One is startled, therefore, when this young man is given moments of unusual vision, and is made to feel deeply and to think imaginatively. The combination could be made convincing (Mansie living a secret inner life and showing a conventional face to the world, as Muir says he did himself in Glasgow), but it is not. The distance between sensitive, intelligent narrator and commonplace character set up at the beginning is continually being narrowed and then, when the author guiltily remembers he is writing a novel, widened again. That Mansie is more interesting than for consistency he should be is the novel's major defect, and one of the chief things that make it worth reading.

The other characters are seen externally. Muir shows great intelligence and psychological insight in describing a character, but not the true novelist's ability to make a character live and speak with an individual voice. He writes a penetrating sketch of David Brand when introducing him (69-75), but then does little with him. The one important woman character, Helen Williamson, is seen entirely from the points of view of the two brothers, has no independent life.

Muir's genius was not for novel-writing. Nevertheless his intelligence, sensitivity and vision make this book far more interesting and moving than most novels. Four big themes are combined – love, politics, death and religion – and the strands are skilfully interwoven. The first is the least satisfyingly treated; here the failure to create consistent and living characters is most damaging. But even here there are moments of

poetic feeling. Mainly Muir uses Mansie's relationship with girls to comment on attitudes to
sex in urban, puritan communities, but occasionally he strikes down to a deeper level, when
Mansie and Helen are shown experiencing
something approaching real love. 'Beneath them
the sea's surface ran smooth and unbroken to the
opposite shore several miles away. And lying
there they were frozen to the same immobility as
the sea; it was not a frame of flesh and blood but a
transubstantiated body that he clasped' (52).
Their trance-like state looks forward to the
'deepening trance' in which angel and girl meet
in the late poem 'The Annunciation'. What they
here and later (119-24) are said to share makes
one wish for a deeper treatment of their relationship throughout. Mansie's experience in love is
repeated in another context after his conversion
to socialism, during a May Day parade. Again
bodies, this time of the ordinary people around
him, are 'transubstantiated'. It was a religious
rather than a merely political vision, and was to
find its best expression in Muir's work in 'The
Transfiguration'. It is in describing such visions
that the poet Muir speaks, but through Mansie he
gives also some impression of the ordinary life of
Glasgow at that time. Seeing him trying, not
always successfully, to combine the surface and
the deeper levels is one of the chief fascinations
of this novel. Here we have the grittiness of
ordinary life, which some find lacking in the

poetry, and the poet's imaginative vision.

In treating of Tom Manson's long illness and death the real life situation is altered by making Mansie the elder brother and by making him feel responsible for Tom's accident because of his relationship with Helen. The opportunity so created to show inner conflicts in Mansie is not fully exploited. But the illness and death of Tom and the effects on the household are brilliantly described, in greater detail than in the account of Johnnie Muir's death in the AUTOBIOGRAPHY. In whatever proportion 'true' fiction and truth of another kind are here mixed, this strand of the story is presented with convincing realism, compassionately and without sentimentality.

Tom's dying is given extra poignancy by being set in the midst of Mansie's 'emancipation' from religious faith and conversion to socialism. (The order of events in Muir's life was quite different.) This enables the narrator in a fine meditation (231-6) to tie together the political, religious and death themes. For Mansie heaven has been brought down to earth, as the socialist Utopia of the future. Paradoxically this does not bring it closer. It means that those who, like Tom, die before Utopia is reached can never enter it. 'So long as is was in Time, Time would sunder him from it.' But if it could be returned to its place beyond time, 'Time would once more become whole and perfect, and a meaning be given not only to present death, but to all the countless dead lying under their green mounds, so that the living and the dead and the unborn might no longer be separated by Time, but gathered together in Time by an everlasting compact beyond Time.' All Mansie's deepest experiences have pointed towards a reality which, if it could be believed in (no doctrine is stated, the sentence is in the conditional), would give them meaning. The final two chapters bring the book to a clear, if tentative, conclusion, bind it into a whole. Even when using a form which does not completely suit him Muir achieves a rare largeness and wholeness of vision.

Readers new to Muir will be the ones best able to appreciate this book simply as a novel. Others should also be able to enjoy it for itself, as a moving, if uneven, work; and will find extra interest in comparing how similar material is used in it and later in the AUTOBIOGRAPHY and in the poems. For instance, one can compare the longish account of Mansie's going into the room where his dead brother lies and of his thoughts there (POOR TOM, 250-4) with the much shorter corresponding passage in the AUTOBIOGRAPHY (103), and both these with the late poem 'The Brothers'. Though one is likely to conclude that Muir found the right form for his personal memories in straight autobiography and for his deeper self in poetry, POOR TOM is not wholly superceded by later works. The AUTOBIOGRAPHY is a greater book, but in it the mature man is very much in

INTRODUCTION

control. There are parts of POOR TOM which give a more intimate feel of what it was like to be a young man growing up in Glasgow in the early years of this century. The extra detail adds something, and the fuller treatment of sexual experience. Among the most interesting passages special to POOR TOM are two in which Mansie remembers incidents from childhood. In one (110-13) he remembers his relationship with a little girl on a neighbouring farm at the age of six - innocent in itself, yet environed by a sense of guilt and leading on to an account of a phase of acute childish guilt, which is reproduced with modifications in the AUTOBIOGRAPHY (34-5), but without any reference to the girl. The other (170-3) is a memory of Mansie's encounter at the age of twelve with a horse - of the sense of terror, wonder, strangeness. This, I feel, must be from life. In any case it makes an impressive addition to the list of Muir's poems and passages of poetic prose about animals - actual, not fabulous animals. His finest writings do not escape into another world, but convey an intense feeling of the strangeness of the familiar.

POOR TOM was published in 1932 by J. M. Dent, with a book jacket by William Johnstone, who had been instrumental in bringing it to the notice of Richard Church, Dent's poetry editor.

P. H. Butter
Glasgow, 1982

PART ONE

I

WHEN one evening in the early autumn of 1911 Tom Manson saw his brother Mansie coming out with Helen Williamson through the gate of the Queen's Park in Glasgow, he stopped as if he had been given a blow on the chest. He told himself that he must be mistaken; but, no, there was no doubt about it; Mansie and Helen were walking along there like old friends. They had not noticed him, but with their faces turned towards each other went off along the park railings towards Pollokshaws Road. Behind his incredulous rage Tom felt honestly alarmed for them; they were so completely unconscious of their danger; they had no idea that they had been seen! But then, as by the single turn of a screw, his fury completely flooded him, sweeping out everything else. He turned and walked down Victoria Road. " By God, I'll get even with him ! " he thought, but no expedient came to his mind, and his anger took another leap upwards.

He pushed open the swing-door of a pub and went up to the counter. The barmaid smiled at him; he could see that all right; but at the same time it was only a distant glassy re-arrangement of her features, so he paid no attention to it but ordered a double Scotch, and when that was swallowed, a second one which he drank more slowly. His anger now quite filled him, yet when he turned into Garvin Street and neared his home it took another leap upwards, lifted him up with it, so that he seemed to be walking partly on the air. Slamming the house door behind him he made at once for the room where he and Mansie slept and began to haul his clothes and belongings to the parlour. The sound of furniture banging brought his mother from the kitchen.

"What are you doing, Tom?" she cried. "You'll break the bit sticks o' furniture if you're no' careful."

"Leave me alone!"

"But, lamb, what's the matter?"

"If you think I'm going to sleep another night in the same room as that——" He had to stop, for only one word would come to his tongue, and he could not speak it out before his mother. So in revenge he said: "I'm leaving to-morrow. I'm going to ship on the first liner I find."

"But what's wrong, Tom? Tell me what's wrong?"

"Leave me alone!" he shouted. "Can't you leave me alone!"

His mother turned, and her bowed back as she

left the room filled him with despair. No, he would never be able to leave this hole! He was chained here. He went through to the bedroom again and carried his bedclothes to the parlour, threw them on the horsehair sofa, and stood staring at them. A key turned in the outside door, and someone stepped into the lobby. He stood rigidly listening. There were voices in the kitchen and then steps in the lobby; but it was his cousin Jean who entered.

"What idiocy have you been up to now?" she asked. "Do you know that your mother's crying in the kitchen?"

"Leave me alone," said Tom. But now he spoke in a merely sulky voice.

Jean looked at the bedclothes piled on the sofa: "A fine mess you've made. Are you going to sleep here?" Then she turned to him, her voice changing, and asked: "Tom, what has happened?"

"Oh, it's no business of yours." He went across to the window, and looking out said: "Well, if you want to know, Mansie's walking out a lady that used to be a great visitor here at one time. I caught them coming out of the Queen's Park."

"What? Not Helen Williamson?"

"Yes, Helen Williamson."

"But it's absurd! It's impossible!"

"Well, I saw them. Haven't I told you?"

Jean was silent for a moment, then she asked : " Did they see you ? "

" They were too much occupied with each other."

She stood looking at him : " But what's to be done now ? "

" That's not my affair. I'm going to ship on a liner to-morrow."

" Don't talk nonsense. You know you've got to consider your mother. But I never thought Mansie was such a terrible fool as that ! "

" Well, do you expect me to live here after this ? "

Jean stood thinking. Presently she said : " Go for a walk. And I'll make your bed and put this room in some order."

She began at once, turning her back on him. At the door he said : " At any rate, it wasn't my fault this time."

" Who says it was your fault ? " Then she burst out : " That woman will be a curse to the both of you ! I never liked her."

" It's his fault, not hers."

" Do you stick up for her still ? But I don't deny that it's Mansie's fault. I'll have to tell your mother, I suppose."

Tom walked rapidly up Victoria Road. But when he came to the park gates again his rage met him like a wave and turned him automatically in the opposite direction from the one that Mansie and Helen had taken. With his mother and Jean there he would never be able to get back at that creeper. Velvet-heeled creeper! Scented velvet-heeled creeper! Rows of black, spiked railings spun past him, and he struck at them with his stick. Like a prison, these neat streets and numbered houses and genteel railings. Why had his father hauled him back that time when he had tried to run off to sea? He had actually got to Blackness, was on the boat, tucked away all safe in the forecastle; and then his father came, the very skin at the root of his nose white with anger; and he had got out of the ship again and into the cart, and his father had driven him home to the farm, five hopeless miles. He had been sixteen then – a fellow was far too much at the mercy of everybody at sixteen! – and then his father had had his first heart attack, and that had put a stop to all hope of running away to sea. And when his father died there was his mother to look after, for Mansie had done a bunk to Glasgow long before that: the creeper always knew how to sneak out of things. No wonder he had taken to drink when they had gone to Blackness after his father's death; he knew every stone in the streets and hated every one of them; but when you got drunk your nose wasn't brought up against them at every turn; it seemed to give you some hope. Oh, why hadn't they let him go to sea? They hadn't known what they were doing.

He was walking now through a wide park dotted with groups of young men in shirt-sleeves playing football. And as if in response to his release from the constriction of the rows of railed houses, he saw himself again, as he had often seen himself, standing at the prow of an ocean-going ship in the solitary morning watch, standing bare-footed and with uncovered head in the wide flapping trousers and blue jersey of a sailor, a cigarette between his lips, a foreign look, the look of one who has seen many lands, on his face. The circle of the sea horizon rose and sank with a slow turning motion like a great coin lazily spinning, and within that ring of danger he was secure, for danger itself was a shield, turning aside all that was equivocal and treacherous and creeping. Yes, that was the life for him ; but his father had not known and his mother would never know what a thirst a fellow could have for the sea, so that he seemed to choke on dry land, choke as if a dry clod were rammed down his throat. The sea, or the Wild West with a revolver at your side, some place where you knew your friends and your enemies, knew where you stood.

But suddenly, while he was still in mid-ocean, the turn of Helen's neck as she looked up at Mansie rose before him. Damn and blast her ! It was as if she had given him a blow between the eyes, and he, lying on his back in the gutter, were asking her in pure astonishment why she had

done that.   And he would have given up everything for her.   How good he had felt at that party,
the first evening they had met !   But he mustn't
think of that.   Still, when she wouldn't tell him
her address, by God she had been perfectly right !
Better for him if he had never found it out.   A
damned fool, too, to have wandered round
Langside every evening that week in the frost
and cold, among all these new streets, great blocks
of redstone they were, with genteel railed gardens
in front.   Of course he hadn't met her there.   But
on the Sunday he had got up good and early and
gone to the church she attended.   Well, he had
asked for his medicine pretty thoroughly, right
enough.   He had looked all round the church,
but couldn't find her.   He might have given it up
as a bad job then ; but no, he had to wait on the
pavement when the service was over, and after a
while out she came.   He had hardly dared to step
up to her, the soft fool ; he didn't know at that
time that she was the sort that would kiss and
canoodle with anybody.   But it was all easier
than he had expected, far too damned smooth
and easy altogether, and she agreed to go for a
walk in the park with him without winking an
eyelash.   Might as well have given him her
address at the first go off ; but that was like her.
And then it was a long time before he plucked up
his courage and got it out – a nice sunny day it
was, after the frost – but out it came at last : " I

love you." And his voice had trembled : was
there ever such a fool ? It had made her catch
her breath all the same ; but then she had replied
in that superior way of hers : " How can you tell
that ? You don't know me." But he thought he
knew her better than anybody had ever known
a girl, and that began it. Yet even then he
hadn't dared to touch her, or to kiss her, for
weeks and weeks. Still, that had been the
happiest time he had had with her. Better if the
thing had always stayed at that stage. For her
kisses drove a fellow frantic, and she didn't seem
to know it. Flung herself at you and thought
she could go on doing that till the cows came
home ; kissing and nothing more. Thus far and
no farther. And after it was over she would just
pat her hat to rights again, looking as superior
and genteel as ever, and that was that. How
could he have stood it ? No wonder he got
violent that night in Maxwell Park ; he was
beyond himself, he couldn't help it. But then he
had crept and crawled before her, licked her
boots, told her he was a waster, and promised
never to offend again. And after all it wasn't any
use, for she kept as stiff as a poker, never gave
him another chance, took no pity on a fellow.
And now she was kissing and canoodling with
that creeper. By God, if he had guessed that
would ever happen he would have known what
to do ; he would have paid no attention to her

objections ; that was how to treat tarts of her
kind. A proper soft mark he had been.

Now he was among streets again. His anger,
which had winged his feet, now fell like the
sudden ceasing of a wind. He felt tired ; a
drink would do him good. He pushed open the
swing-door of a pub. As he sat drinking, and
the comforting equivocality of alcohol spread
through his mind, he gave himself over more and
more completely to the thought that he was a
waster, as though it were a consoling thought.
It didn't matter what happened to a poor devil
like him ; let them kiss and canoodle. But
then – for even a waster must take some measures
of defence against his enemies – he suddenly saw
that he must get back before Mansie ; it was a
point of honour, a point of honour that a creeper
mightn't understand ; but it would be indecent if
he wasn't home before Mansie, if he wasn't sitting
at home and waiting for him. So Tom got
unsteadily to his feet.

But as he approached Garvin Street a long forgotten memory of his childhood came back to
him. A big lout, the son of a neighbouring
farmer, had lain in wait for Mansie one evening.
Mansie had stood with a terrified look on his
face, refusing to fight ; but Tom, although he
was only a little boy at the time, had flown at
Mansie's tormentor screaming : " You're no' to
hurt Mansie ! You're no' to hurt Mansie ! "

And everybody had laughed, and there had been no fight. And now Mansie had given him a stab in the back. Without provocation. His elder brother that he had always looked up to, that he would have done anything for. " By God, I'll get even with him ! " he said as he went up the stairs, but it was only the repetition of an empty phrase. And when he opened the door he felt so tired that he walked straight through to the parlour – driven out of his very room, by God ! – and forlornly went to bed.

After a long and inconclusive debate with his mother in the kitchen, Mansie wearily betook himself to his room. He had denied that there was anything between himself and Helen, denied it as indignantly as if he were speaking the truth ; and indeed what he had told her was partly true at least, entirely true in fact if you only counted the time up to the moment when, yielding to a silly impulse – it had become far too much of a habit with him, dash it ! – he had stooped down and kissed Helen on the mouth. He knew it was a mistake the minute it was done, knew it as soon as he found her in his arms, knew it while her lips were still clinging to his : a silly goat to have got himself into such a fix for the sake of a moment's pleasure. But then, whether it was the total abandon with which Helen fell into his arms, as if she had been fatefully poised in a perilous equilibrium that only one touch was needed to destroy, or whether it was the slightly terrifying thought that this was Tom's girl, whom it would be wicked to trifle with, almost blasphemous to embrace unless one were driven by an irresistible passion that excused everything : all at once they had both become serious, they had looked at each other like conspirators suddenly bound together by a fatal act that they had not foreseen a moment before, revealing them to each other in a flash, so that it would have been useless, even perverse, to pretend any longer. This wasn't like his other affairs with girls at all ! The frightening thought had shot through Mansie's mind while Helen's lips were still pressed to his. There was no turning back now. A serious business !

And now, as he lit the gas-jet in his room, he thought again, listening involuntarily for any sound from the parlour where Tom was lying : A serious business ! But all the same what he had told his mother was true. Helen had only come to him for help and advice. And besides, it was a dashed shame of Tom to have lain in wait for her, stopping her and speaking to her like that : the poor girl was frightened out of her wits and didn't know where to turn. Tom should have taken his dismissal like a man. Why, it was two months now since she had told him that it was all over between them ! And yet the fellow still went on persecuting her, even stopping her in the street : that was carrying things a bit too far. Still it was dashed unfortunate that Tom had seen them that evening. It was like him, all the same ; always stumbling against things that hurt him, always getting himself and other people into trouble. Well, he had only himself to blame ; Helen would never have had him back whatever happened.

Mansie glanced round the bedroom. It had a strange naked look. Made a fellow feel quite queer, that empty iron bedstead ; something ugly and threatening about it. Things would be dashed uncomfortable in the house now, with Tom in that state of mind. Mansie slowly took off his clothes. Unpleasant going to bed with that thing standing there by the wall as if it were watching you. Wish Bob Ryrie were here to keep a fellow company. Bob would be able to advise one too. He turned his back on the bedstead. A serious business ! And he was to see Helen on Saturday afternoon. He almost wished now that he had not fixed up that appointment with her ; but there was no drawing back ; the damage was done ; Tom had seen them, and there would be no use in trying to convince him that——

Putting out the gas, Mansie slipped into bed, carefully avoiding the iron bedstead still reproachfully

and threatingly exposing its shameful nakedness
to him in the light of the street lamp outside.
For a long time he lay awake thinking of Helen
and Tom and wishing that Bob Ryrie were there
with him. He felt forsaken and unjustly treated,
like a child locked as a punishment in an empty
room where damaged and disused pieces of
furniture are kept. But at last he fell asleep.

2

Since there's no hope, come let us kiss . . .

DRAYTON.

IF TOM MANSON had had the ability to crystallise his vague feelings of betrayal connected with Glasgow he might have said that he was betrayed by a kiss. For it was a kiss, or rather a special kind of kiss, known perhaps only in Puritan countries which have been thoroughly industrialised without being civilised to the point requisite for an industrialised population, that was one of the chief causes of his later misfortunes.

Like all born lovers of freedom Tom had always been irked by a countless number of things which tamer natures adapt themselves to without inconvenience. His father's farm had irked him because it was stationary, because the seasons followed one another, because the soil had to be ploughed and the harvest reaped; and the little town of Blackness had begun to irk him as soon as he felt that he knew every stone in it. For on the farm he had at least felt the horizon round him wherever he went; but here his sight was bounded by arbitrary walls, and if he got drunk oftener than he should it was partly because then the houses lost their stability, rocked lightly like ships at anchor, and seemed on the point of floating away ; and this fluctuating barrier was far more endurable than the rigid walls that sobriety raised about him. Sometimes as he walked home at night after a spree he would kick a particularly massive stone in the wall, at first to convince himself that it was as solid as it looked, and finally in anger at its unresponsiveness. Next day his imprisonment was always harder to bear.

When at last his apprenticeship in the engineering shop was over and he could go to Glasgow, the hugeness of that city became an image of inexhaustible freedom. For a year he was enchanted by the variety and strangeness of Glasgow. Even the unfamiliar conventions pleased him, and he set himself eagerly to acquire them. And although he came from a northern island where people's speech had still a ballad frankness and young men still climbed in through their sweethearts' windows at night, he soon learned what words might and might not be addressed to a respectable young Glasgow typist. Like almost everybody, indeed, who, coming from a relatively primitive state of society, seeks to adapt himself to one that is more complex, he made the error of taking the new

conventions at their face value and fell from his
natural frankness into a fantastic propriety. One
thing in particular helped to make his attitude to
women excessively correct. A man who has been
accustomed to steal to his sweetheart under cover
of night insensibly comes to associate love with
loosened hair on pillows and matches clandes-
tinely struck, and the sight of a young lady,
correctly dressed, walking towards him through
the crowd, which he has been watching for the
last ten minutes, awakens in him quite a different
train of thoughts and conducts him into a world
from which there is no bridge to the world of love
as he has known it. And that bridge being un-
thinkable, he comes in time to conceive of the
transition to the physical rites of love as a perfectly
arbitrary step not provided for by the convention,
a blind leap out of one world into another, a
violent settlement of a question for which there is
no legitimate solution. Tom, in other words,
simply could not imagine himself lying in bed
with the stylishly dressed girls whom he walked
out – at least while he was walking them out ; or
rather he could not imagine the process which
would lead to that consummation : day and night
attire having for him almost the force of two
absolute conditions – the present in which he was
embedded, and the past from which he had been
roused for ever. And even when he fell in love
with Helen his feelings still remained in this

suspended state, and it was only when she granted him a little more than he had reckoned upon that Glasgow and its conventions began to irk him : the small draught of freedom repre- sented by a special kind of kiss was enough to make him feel his bonds.

They must have kissed sooner or later ; but while in the world which Tom had known an ardent kiss was only the prelude to a more inti- mate caress, to Helen it seemed to be the end. And the passion with which she flung herself upon it had something of despair and renuncia- tion. It was as though in a fury of make-believe she hoped to transform it without anyone's knowledge, even her own, into that ultimate surrender which she allowed to enter her imagina- tion only as a legendary happening. To Tom this final and sterile kiss, rehearsed so often, gave a momentary appeasement, an appeasement which was half torture, however, for it seemed to have so little meaning ; it was followed by a feeling of apprehension which he could not shake off. It was as though he had gone with Helen into the house of love, thinking at first : This is only the ante-room, but presently discovering that it was the only chamber in the house. For though there is another door in the inner wall of this room so much frequented by young couples in the larger towns of Scotland, a door leading presumably to other chambers, when one examines it one finds that it is only painted, very realistically, on the wall. There is even, it may be, a handle affixed to this door, but if there is, the handle is false too, it turns round and round accommodatingly as long as one chooses to turn it, but nothing happens : it is wooden, the ante-room is wooden, the whole house is wooden, a long narrow wooden shell with a splendid façade. Behind this façade, in such a long and shallow room, Tom and Helen performed their passionate and sterile rites.

Yet at certain moments, when two lovers strain against the painted door, there must come, no matter how convincingly their conscience assures them of the contrary, the urgent knowledge that the door is real after all, that other rooms lie beyond it, and that if they could awaken they might find themselves, with fear and trembling, but with definite relief, ensconced there. And while to all appearances they are quite happy in the bright room, and feel privileged to be there, in secret they are thinking of those other chambers whose existence they never admit to each other, and which have become a subterranean domain through which their thoughts can licentiously roam while they stand so chastely clasped. In time their embraces become merely a device to gain them admittance to that place, where they can wander in solitary thought, and where, if they ever met, they could not greet each other. So as they stand pressed so closely they are as far apart

as secret drinkers indulging their craving in
shameful privacy. Once, it is true, when desire
first threw them together, they gave themselves
when they kissed, but now, while still pretending
to give, they are merely filching from each other
something they are ashamed of and wish to hide.
So when she casts herself into his arms with the
splendid gesture of one who surrenders everything, offering her breasts to him as though each
were a precious gift which he must accept with
homage, she is merely making a breach in her own
body through which that secret world may break
in and become a private garden where she can
wander at her pleasure, but where she has no
further need of him, where indeed he would be a
burdensome intruder, now that he has been the
means through which she has found her way into
it. And when she kisses him she closes her eyes
as though to hide something, and if she could she
would conceal her face as well, for she cannot
keep the waves of passion from flowing over it,
from rippling under that smooth mask like the
muscles under the hide of some lovely animal.

Such secret pleasures are exciting, but they
leave a sense of guilt towards the object that was
employed to produce them. Tom was filled with
shame that such thoughts should come into his
mind when he was with Helen, and told himself that he was a waster. He felt that he had
desecrated their love, and the fact that she did

not know it made his treachery only the worse.
Yet sometimes, almost drowned by his self-
reproaches, a feeling that he had been betrayed
would rise in him; and then the country girls
that he had lain with, frank whether in conferring
or refusing their favours, would seem to him
innocent compared with this Glasgow girl,
superior as she was to them, and unassailable as
was her virtue. And if they had been within
reach he would have gone to them to be cured.

But, although he observed them, the conventions of the city were still strange to him, and so
he accepted this as one of them. Certainly it
seemed a queer arrangement that young fellows
courting should go about for years with their
senses aroused under their clothes and pay no
more attention to it than to a slight physical
inconvenience, a corn or an attack of indigestion.
But no doubt they got used to it; perhaps it was
a normal drawback of love that had to be
accepted with the rest; still it was queer to think
of so many of them, dressed in their best, bow
ties neatly in place, every button fastened,
trousers creased, and all the time—— The
Rabelaisian picture, comic and yet sordid, im-
printed a sheepish grin on his mouth whenever
he realised that he was one of that ignominious
army. It was a quite definite sense of solidarity,
and although it humiliated him it gave him a
satisfaction as of revenge, though on what or

whom he could not have said. It was unpleasant
to remember Helen at those times.

But to Helen those limitations of love were far
less irksome. As she climbed the stairs, turned the
key in the door of her lodgings, lit the gas in her
room and absently looked round her, she still
breathed that richer atmosphere which the touch
of Tom's lips and arms had distilled, an atmosphere that she inhaled effortlessly through every
pore of her body, giving her a dreamful sense of
lightness. It was only when she was undressing,
still in a dream, that the weight of her body began
to return ; and the undoing of her corsets, and
all the trifling acts of liberation which had to be
accomplished before she could lie outstretched
in bed, were like a series of infinitely complicated
petty problems that she could never hope to
solve. When at last she lay between the smooth
sheets, every inch of her body seemed weighed
down by a separate burden, lay there dead and
impenetrable, a foreign load attached to her, a
trunk which was of no further use, for it had
been ethereally decapitated ; and her lips, on
which the savour of Tom's kisses was slowly
fading, seemed alone to harbour any life, seemed
alone dedicated to love, a solitary beacon in the
darkness. When she turned on her other side
for relief it seemed an ignominious thing that
she had to turn all her body ; it was a conscious
and deliberate act that was shameful and also

in some way perilous. And she plunged into sleep like a stone falling into an abyss.

Sensual images came to her very seldom, but when they did they were brutally vivid. She saw Tom before her stripped naked, his head cropped like a boxer's, his flesh leaden. But worst of all were the times when his nakedness was persistently obstructed by some trifle, a collar fastened by a stud round his neck, or a sock on one foot ; for that was like a dismemberment, as though the collar severed his head from his shoulders and the sock darkly conjured his foot away. These startling materialisations terrified her at the rare moments when she remembered them, and it seemed impossible that she should have seen or imagined them – she, the girl who stood in the ante-chamber of love.

It is in the hand that the human will is most unequivocally incarnated, so unequivocally, in-deed, that we are often held responsible even for its involuntary motions. So when Tom raised his hand and almost imperceptibly touched Helen's breast, that breast which so often had been flung at him by the blind engine of her body, crushed against his so firmly and long that he could hear the beating of her heart ; when he raised his hand to those softly outlined spheres, the act had all the appearance of deliberate violation, of Luciferian blasphemy. She was so outraged and incredulous that he at once

stammered an apology. Finally she forgave him,
but that was the beginning of their rupture. For
when she had crushed her breasts against him it
had been in involuntary obedience to the com-
pulsion that threw their bodies – no, perhaps not
even their bodies – that threw their souls together. And although she was perfectly conscious of the thrill of the impact, and indeed
enjoyed it secretly and deliberately, yet no action
takes on the indelible stamp of responsibility
until it is acknowledged by some other human
being; indeed until then one cannot even be
sure that it ever happened; and Tom gave no
sign, perhaps he had not noticed. Helen was
too absorbed in her inner sensations, however,
for such questions to present themselves to her
except in the vaguest terms. But when Tom
raised his hand against her breast as though
against herself the cloud was torn asunder; she
felt naked, and she could not fling herself into his
arms again in such complete obliviousness of
what she was doing. It was after this that she
began to dream of Tom without his clothes.

3

WHILE Tom dreamt of adventures, Mansie's reveries were filled with hosts of friends, and his most comforting thought was that with the years their numbers would increase. Yet he never took the first step ; he merely held himself expectantly open, and this of itself was enough to tell anyone who met him that here was a real friendly fellow, and to put the more sensitive into a position in which an advance into intimacy was unavoidable. But nobody except undesirable people ever wanted to escape the tacit invitation. Mansie was like one of those actresses to whom bouquets seem to fly of their own accord, and to him each new friendship was indeed a sort of bouquet which he accepted without affectation, privately conscious that he deserved it, but far too decent a fellow to let the slightest sign of this appear. His life was passed among his friends as in a garden exhaling an almost sensible fragrance and warmth ; and it filled him with pleasure to know that no corner was uncultivated, and to look forward for a whole week, aware that every evening he would be in some sheltered arbour of this pleasance which expanded in an ever wider concentric ring as the years went on and yet remained intimate, resembling a private estate.

The thing that puzzled him most was how he had got on so well in life, how he had come to be promoted over the heads of men older and more pushing than himself, and he was occasionally troubled by the thought : could he be a sly fellow after all, sly perhaps without knowing it ? But these thoughts came to him only in moods of dejection : they were really too absurd. Next morning he would contemplate his business career half in wonder and half in gratitude, and acknowledge frankly how lucky he had been, for his popularity with his employers and with the customers was pure luck ! And fortune itself seemed then the paragon of decent fellows, and he cherished for it, though invisible, exactly the feelings one decent fellow cherishes for another who has done him a good turn.

It was somewhat the same feeling that had led to his conversion and his membership of the Baptist Chapel. This had happened a little after he came to Glasgow. There had been a great revival, several men in the warehouse had been accepted by Christ, and Mansie, already so popular with decent fellows, felt assured that he could not be turned away. Perhaps too he was afraid that he might be missing an opportunity of bettering himself, and this was a point on which his conscience was really strict; for bettering himself was associated in his mind with disagreeable effort, with such things as asking the manager for an increase of salary, and to evade such difficulties made him almost fear that he might be a man of weak character. So he went to the revival meeting and was quietly saved. Afterwards he was very glad he had done so, for the uprush of ecstatic feeling that followed had taken him quite by surprise, and again he felt that gratitude, this time tinged with a degree of awe, which one decent fellow feels for another who has done him a good turn.

He read very little, contenting himself with the *Glasgow Herald* and the *British Weekly*, and did not regard himself as a " literary fellow "; yet he would have been distressed to be found wanting in reverence for things which were deserving of it, and when the Reverend John McKail in his sermon one Sunday quoted, as though in independent confirmation of his own views, " God's in His Heaven, All's right with the world," Mansie felt that there must be something in this fellow Browning and in poetry too, although from all he had heard it was a rather profane business; and picking up *Great Thoughts* one day from the desk of one of the clerks in the office, and finding in it extracts in verse from great names, such as Tennyson, Browning, Coventry Patmore and Dante, extracts in which encouraging

counsels were expressed in perfectly understandable words, he nodded his head in appreciation of those great men who could descend for a
little while from their " poetry," and say something to help a simple fellow like himself. That
was true Christianity. Over one of the sentences,
not in verse, he actually chuckled : " Hitch your
wagon to a star." What things those great writers
thought of ! He would have to tell Bob Ryrie
that one.

He was as nice in his habits as in his taste for
literature. A spot of dirt on his sleeve was
enough to make him unhappy, and when occasionally he went out for a country walk for the
sake of his health, he always came back, no matter
how muddy the roads were, with his black shoes
speckless. Clumsiness in others annoyed him ;
so that whenever Tom returned at night with
another wound, the sight of the bloody bandage
smeared with oil and grit angered him and sent
a thin rush of blood, as though in resentful
answer, to his own cheeks ; and somewhere
in his mind the words took shape : " Great
clumsy brute ! " For it was all so unnecessary !
To live and dress quietly was simple enough, one
would have thought, and it wasn't as if he ap-
proved of display, or put a rose in his buttonhole
except when he was going to meet a girl. He
liked his suits to be of a soft shade of fawn, his
neckties to be quiet ; and if his circular stiff

collar was smooth as glass and white as snow, and his circular bowler hat had the burnished sparkle of good coal, and his shoes were impeccable, he felt he need fear nobody. Yet he disapproved of the travellers who put on a la-di-da Kelvinside accent; that was going too far altogether; and although he tried to speak correctly, in what he took to be English, he kept something plain and unassuming in the intonation: for it would have seemed to him offensive presumption to pretend to be anything but an ordinary fellow like anybody else. And besides it was only decent to the English language to pronounce it as it was spelt.

A young man, good-looking and neatly dressed, who sets out conspicuously to be decent to everybody, will be greeted with decency on every side; the world surrounding him will obediently turn into the world of his imagination, and in that world, if his own decency and his faith in the decency of others are sufficiently strong or blind, he may live secluded as in a soft prenatal reverie for a long time, and if he is fortunate for all his life. Mansie lived in such a world, and except for an occasional harsh echo from the tremendous world outside he was happy in it. Tom was the most constant jarring presence, but being constant, allowance could be made for him, and the disturbance, if not avoided, yet foreseen. The only serious threat to Mansie's happiness came from those moments, and they were infrequent, when he found himself morally in the wrong. That this should happen seemed to him not only undeserved, but even unnatural, and then he could be very harsh on whatever acquaintance might happen to threaten the inviolate image of his decency. He had, however, a happy capacity for forgetting things; he could forget Tom while he was actually talking to him; and he forgot those other disagreeable moments so completely that, searching his mind, it would have been difficult for him to remember that anybody had ever accused him of an action even slightly incorrect.

And how quietly and yet intensely happy was his life! When, returning in the evening in the tramcar from the semi-exile of the day, he saw his friends like a glorified host awaiting him, friends to whom for the calm rest of the evening he could devote himself, sometimes it seemed too much, and a lump would rise in his throat. But recollection gave him a joy almost as intense; for instance when he remembered the moments that big Bob Ryrie laid his scrubbed and scented hand on his sleeve, and, his face as near as a girl's, put him up to some business tip; then the memory of the urgent affection in Bob's voice and eyes would fill him with embarrassment, and he would feel almost as though he had listened to a love declaration. Often, thinking of the way in which

Bob inclined his head as they walked slowly side by side, in Mansie's mind a very early and apparently inconsequent memory would rise, the memory of a picture of the disciples in a child's Life of Jesus which his mother had read to him ; and there one of the disciples was shown with his head lying on another's breast. Somewhere in Mansie's mind was the definite knowledge that the other figure was Jesus Himself, yet as Bob was confused with this recollection the idea that it should have been Jesus was in some way blasphemous ; and it seemed to him a more reverent thought that the second man had been merely a disciple. And while he was dreamily absorbed in this thought, his business round would suddenly appear a sort of pilgrimage, and he himself a humble disciple doing good to people. A real nice fellow, Bob, anyway.

Yet although Bob was so good a friend, something in Mansie shrank from according him more than the privilege of one friend among many ; for he had a profound need to diffuse painlessly in an ever wider concentric circle every impulse within him that was urgent or painful, to vaporise himself hygienically without leaving any muddy residue ; and to do this he needed many friends. There is one impulse, however, that is so palpably localised in the body that all the arts of the vaporiser must fail ; and like most single young men living in a Puritan country, Mansie was

sometimes hard beset by sex. He tried to fight it,
he vaporised heroically ; nevertheless there were
hours in which, most incomprehensibly and
undeservedly, his mind was besieged by lascivious
images, and it was during one of those periods
that he went, at Bob Ryrie's suggestion, to an
address for men only at the Southern P.S.A.
He never went back again, and for some time
there was a slight coldness between Bob and him.
The Wesleyan parson had talked so much about
" control " that Mansie had not known where to
look ; then the word " sex " had rolled roundly
and often through the church, followed by the
Biblical term " seed " – and that was really
going a bit too far ; it had almost turned his
stomach. And in the back seat of the gallery a
crowd of young boys – hooligans they must have
been – had sniggered so much that at last the
preacher, getting quite red about the gills –
Mansie could not understand how that vulgar
expression had leapt so nimbly to his tongue –
had had to rebuke them for their " filthy
minds." These Glasgow people were really a
funny lot.

But soon after this, before the impression left
by the P.S.A. had faded, unexpected relief
arrived. At the Y.M.C.A. Sunday afternoon
meeting he had admired a girl secretly for a long
time, glancing across at her where she sat among
the other girls under the long row of windows at

the opposite side of the hall. Yet he had never dared to speak to her, for obviously she was a superior girl, perhaps even a school-teacher. She was tall and dark, and her clothes had a ruthless perfection of cut; and individually all those things daunted him. Then one day he caught sight of her approaching on the pavement, and when half-defensively and half-hopefully he put up his hand to his hat she smiled and stopped. And in a few moments he found that they had arranged to go for a walk that evening.

It was the last Saturday of the Glasgow Fair. The city had that spacious look which is given to great masses of stone when the cares within them are suspended; the very houses seemed to be breathing a more rarefied atmosphere (perhaps it was merely that no smoke was ascending from the chimneys), the children's shouts rose with unusual clearness, and even the regular boozers who on this vacant Saturday night got drunk because after all it was a Saturday night, seemed forlorn and ineffectual figures wandering about in a mere dream of intoxication which they were striving to make real: in vain, for the sober crowds whose presence alone can prove beyond doubt to a man that he is drunk had inexplicably melted away. On this one Saturday night in the year a drunken man wandering through the solitary streets, where the summer evening still lingers, may carry on for a long time a peaceful

metaphysical debate with himself and at the end
of it not know whether he is drunk or sober;
and finally he will go to bed more in perplexity
than anger, yet with the indefinable feeling that
the world has changed.

Mansie and Isa took the tram to Maxwell
Park, from which they intended to walk to the
Pollok Estate. On the top of the tram, which was
almost empty, Mansie felt, as he always did when
he was committed for the evening to a single
companion, a doubly vivid consciousness of all
the friends whom he had left behind and whose
company he was in a sense sacrificing, and a
trace of bitterness came over him at this girl for
being the cause of such a separation, a trace so
faint, however, that presently it passed into the
resolve to get all the enjoyment he could out of
the evening. The paths and woods of the Pollok
Estate were deserted, and the sense that he was
walking here almost alone with this girl intensi-
fied the pleasurable feeling which Mansie received
from nature, a feeling compounded of a vague
melancholy and a solid conviction of religious
comfort. After he had carefully spread out the
light raincoat that he always carried with him in
provenance, they sat down on the grass behind a
line of bushes which screened them from the road.
Mansie generally kissed, at some suitable moment,
the girls he took for a walk. The moment
came, he kissed Isa, and then the dreadful thing

happened. What was this woman after? Was
this a way for human beings to behave? As
if fleeing from violation the trees and bushes
around him that had stood tranced as if in
anticipation of the coming Sabbath receded to a
remote distance, leaving him to his fate. . . .
Yet the worst moment of all came when,
turning away awkwardly on his side, he had
to readjust his clothes, while behind him he
heard a surreptitious rustling. Yes, she could be
as discreet now as she liked, he might pretend that
he was only brushing the dust from his coat :
nothing could hide the vulgarity of this final end ;
and he felt as though he had been transported
among the working classes, who sat about collar-
less and in their shirt-sleeves, and washed themselves down to the waist at the kitchen sink
while the rest of the family sat at the table eating,
and the word " proletariat," which Brand was so
fond of using, came into his mind, an ugly and
yet meaningless-sounding word. A rush of
unavailing pity for his defenceless clothes, which
had been so rudely violated, almost blasphemed
against, came over him ; and he was sorry for
hers too. To treat a beautiful summer frock like
that showed an insensitive, almost a brutal nature.
What need had she for pretty clothes, if this was
all she wanted ? Any shawlie in the streets was
better dressed for it.

Isa had got to her feet and said curtly : " Well,

are you coming?" The light seemed to have
faded very quickly: how long had they been
lying there? They walked side by side and in
silence between the vague trees. Now and then
he flicked an invisible speck of dust from his coat
sleeve. Suddenly the terrible fear fell upon him
that his bowler hat might have lost its polish,
might even have been dinted; and he took it
from his head and anxiously ran his palm round it.
His clothes seemed to sit less well on him; he
put his hand up to his necktie and was surprised
to find it in place; but his shoes, he knew it for
a certainty, must be covered with dust, and a
feeling of despair came over him, and he said
under his breath: "Well, they'll just have to
wait till I get home."

The security of home for a moment floated
before him, but the sinking at his heart had already
forewarned him before the dreadful question
leapt to his mind: How could he face his mother
now? He saw himself stealing into the house,
having walked about until he knew she would be
in bed; and he would have to forgo her welcoming smile to-night when he was so much in
need of it. Even the cleansing of his shoes from
this dust, the witness of his delinquency, would
no longer be a symbolical act, emblem of his
nicety and the purity of his house, but a sordid
utilitarian stratagem to conceal his transgression
from his mother, and from Tom too, for Tom

would exult in his fall. Suddenly the thought
" Tom has done this " shot through his mind,
and an indeterminate and yet vehement gust of
anger rose into his throat – anger which demanded a direction and clamoured to be fed, and
which he deliberately fed now with the thought
(though he knew it to be false) that Tom had
tricked him into this, that Tom had in some
way by his evil communications caused him to do
this. Tom probably liked it ; with his low pas-
sions he would. And the feeling that Tom had
done what he himself had just done was a greater
affliction, and gave him a deeper sense of degradation, than the impure act itself ; and suddenly he
remembered, as something which he had no
longer any right to remember, his mother laying
her hand on his head, after her Sunday reading
from the child's Life of Christ, and saying :
" That's my good boy."

And how was he to face all the fellows and girls
he knew ? They were walking now along the
railings of Maxwell Park, and he was glad that
night had fallen, for his appearance seemed to
have shrunk, had grown tarnished and mean, and
every time his knees bent there was something
abject in the jack-knife-like action of the joints.
If Bob Ryrie were only here with him instead of
this girl ! The picture of the disciple laying his
head on the other's breast floated up as from a
drowning sea of shapes trying to smother it and

sank again, leaving Mansie's head slightly inclined, as though in desperation he were resting it on the soft evening air. And assemblies of young men in clean raiment and with brushed hair, at Y.M.C.A.s and Bible Classes and Christian Endeavour meetings, appeared in his mind row upon row : there in those decent ranks he would be secure, there he would be clean.

By now they had come within reach of the lighted tramcar at the terminus, and as Mansie stepped into the diffused glassy radiance from the windows he shrank for a moment as if stung. Isa climbed the stairs without turning to look at him, yet she was careful that her long skirts should not float out behind and disclose any glimpse of her ankles. Well, he had seen a lot more than her ankles, he thought, shocked at his own sudden cynicism. Yet, sitting now in the lighted tram, she looked so proud and unapproachable that what had happened that evening seemed a blasphemous impossibility, and when, seeing the conductor approaching, she said coldly, " I get off at Strathbungo," it sounded like a reproof of his disrespectful thoughts, and he felt like a servant receiving an order, and hastily thrust his hand into his pocket for the coppers. Nothing he could do now, not even the simplest action, that did not seem vulgar ! She was like those nurses, he thought. And he remembered the hospital where his friend had lain, and where the nurses had had just that same insolent and distant look. Yet his friend had told him that they were ready for anything, and knew all about a chap, and quite callously exploited their knowledge, and had as little respect for the decency of the human body as an engineer had for the works of a machine. And they smoked too. Did she smoke? he was wondering, when her voice startled him : " Have you lost your tongue, Mr. Manson ? " The impudence ! He could not keep the blood from flushing his face, although he knew she was looking at him. " That's my business ! " he rapped out, but she merely turned away her head with insulting slowness and looked out through the window. Just like a nurse. When the Strathbungo stop came in sight he got up silently to let her out, and silently made to follow her, but when she reached the top of the stairs – they were alone in the tramcar, and only the conductor could hear – she turned and said : " I don't need your company any further, thanks. Good night." And she disappeared.

" All right, then ! All right ! " Mansie exclaimed to the vacant lighted seats in front of him. And after a while, when the tram was already slowing down for the next stop : " Good riddance ! "

Yet after all he did not feel any discomfort when he met his mother that night, nor indeed when he saw Bob Ryrie and his other friends next

day. For one moment when he was left alone
in the tramcar, the thought – which seemed to
have deliberately bided its time until that woman
had gone – the appalling thought, How could he,
a professing Christian and a Sunday-school
teacher, face his God after this ? had risen up
before him and seemed to fill the lighted top of
the tram, which for a moment had a glassier look
than ever. Yet the fact that God already knew
comforted him in some way and made his offence
seem more ordinary. And an ardent plea for
forgiveness that night freed him with extraordinary ease from his distress. And when he
met Bob Ryrie next evening he was surprised to
discover within himself, instead of shame and
embarrassment, a secret sense of condescension.
He even mentioned casually the name of Isa
Smith. What sort of a girl was she ?

Bob leant towards him and said earnestly :
" Don't you have anything to do with her,
Mansie; I know about her. She'll go the full
length with any fellow, and when it's over that's
the last he'll see of her. Queer ! Gets them to the
point, and then looks clean through them the next
time she meets them in the street ! "

Mansie met her a few weeks later, and she did
in fact look through him. " Just as if she'd scored
off me ! " he fumed. " The other way about, I
think, my dear girl ! "

Yet it was Isa who had scored, for Mansie had

fallen, and she had only fallen again. The celerity
too with which he had got rid of his remorse,
while it eased his mind, disquieted him at the
same time. What sort of a fellow could he be not
to feel up or down after committing a sin like
that? And sometimes to reassure himself he
would again ask God's pardon, though he could
never feel sure that this might not be an act of
presumption against God, an indirect reflection
on God for having forgiven him so quickly, and
for so completely having removed any trace of
remorse. Almost like over-complaisance, almost
like collusion! The very thought, the very
thought of such a thought, was blasphemous,
and now Mansie really did not know for what he
should pray to God, nor in what terms his prayer
could be couched. Yet his soul seemed to be
begging him for something that he could not
give it.

The other effect of his offence was more practi-
cally difficult to deal with. For he knew now that
he could get relief – and with alarming ease – from
the stress of desire, and so he was no longer
safely enclosed within his own confusion and
torment of mind : the door of temptation stood
wide open. Girls, even the most faultlessly
dressed, even the most unapproachable and nurse-
like, were accessible. During the next few years,
in spite of an unwearied fight, Mansie fell more
than once and less involuntarily than the first

time. And curiously enough he too, like Isa,
could never afterwards bear the sight of his
partners in guilt. To have continued such
connections would have seemed to him indecent.
How a fellow could deliberately, with his eyes
open, go on associating with a girl after it had
happened once – planning out their indulgence,
perhaps even unblushingly talking it over together ! – he simply could not understand such
a thing. But if it were always with a different
girl it might be called unpremeditated at least, in
fact almost a surprise ; and if one fell always
with a different girl, it was in a way a first fall
every time. And the ease with which one
obtained forgiveness was almost uncanny.

Yet now and then Mansie still felt the lack of
the remorse that would not come. It was as
though there was a vacuum within his soul, and
at its centre, completely insulated and quite
beyond reach, a tiny point of pain.

As he lay thinking of the past evening and
involuntarily glancing every now and then at the
iron skeleton of the forsaken bed, the memory of
that first hour of guilt haunted him, and it was
as though something far within his mind, so far
within that he could not reach it or stop what it
was doing, was trying to weave some connection
between Isa and Helen. He had the feeling, at

any rate, that something was being woven, something implicating him and yet beyond his control, and the words shot through his mind, " I'm in for it ! " as he thought of Saturday, when he was to meet Helen. And he knew that he would go to the appointed meeting-place in spite of everything, of the scandal, of Tom, of his mother and Jean, and of the opinion of all good fellows.

4

But ye loveres, that bathen in gladnesse,
If any drope of pitee in yow be,
Remembreth yow on passed hevinesse
That ye han felt, and on the adversitee
Of othere folk.

CHAUCER.

THEY caught sight of each other at the same instant; twenty yards of the Central Station separated them. People hurrying to their trains, message-boys, porters, crossed the line stretched between his eyes and hers, but it did not waver, and as he walked straight towards her he seemed to be following a beautiful and exact course which cut through the aimless crowd as through smoke and only reached its end when it joined his hand and hers. At first, when they were too far off to read each other's faces, their eyes had been filled with doubt and questioning; but now love had risen round them and enclosed them like a wall, and within that perfect security they could once more look questioningly at each other, no longer with dread, as a few moments before, but with delight at the thought of the strangeness which it was their reciprocal right to explore. And so keen was their desire to do so that the suddenly arisen citadel of love within which they now stood became an objective fact whose consideration they could calmly postpone.

But the joy of discovery had also to be postponed when presently they found themselves in a crowded third-class compartment of the Gourock train. Helen sat in the corner, Mansie sat beside her ; they were silent and gazed out through the window, scarcely seeing the things that fleeted past their eyes : the backs of sooty tenement buildings with washing clouts hanging out to dry from kitchen windows, the neat red-gravelled suburban stations sweeping smoothly past as if on runners, sharp bridges, coal trucks, a red factory wall. But when, after Paisley, the train ran through the flat farm-country, and they saw the yellow cornfields half-reaped, and the red and yellow woods, they felt that it was for them that nature had transformed itself in this strange and brilliant way, for the last time they had seen the country it had been an ordinary green. Now everything was dry and bright ; the stubble fields glistened, the ancient castle of Dumbarton on its rock across the river seemed to give out an infinitesimal sparkle as of impalpable dust, the jewelled leaves rested on nothing more solid than the air, were held in it as in a translucent crystal, and the trunks and branches of dried

wood rose unencumbered, as if they no longer felt
the weight of their shining burden. Yet this
aridity was not that of barrenness ; the dust on
the roads beside the railway lines seemed as rich
as seed, and the coloured leaves fell ceaselessly as
though they wanted to bury the earth. At
Langbank gardens with rows of deep and
bright yellow flowers flashed by, then the inky
tenements of Port Glasgow passed, almost
unseen, before their eyes, and Greenock rotting
patiently between the beautiful hills and the
majestic firth. Nevertheless when they emerged
from the stifling tunnel, and for a moment the
estuary of the Clyde flashed upon them like a
turning mirror before the train ran into Gourock
station, they felt as though an oppression had
been lifted.

Yet now that they walked along it, they scarcely
saw the estuary outstretched like a great blue
stone, nor the near houses, nor the dark hills on
the opposite shore ; for the desire to know and
make known had again taken possession of
them, and they reached the end of the long and
empty promenade as though it had melted into
air before them, so open were their minds to each
other, and so vivid were the images that they contemplated there. They felt that they must know
everything, but still more strongly that they
must tell everything ; for in the suspended calm
which preludes desire, a calm in which passion

is so subtly diffused that it is bodiless, they had
been so transmuted that they were conscious of
nothing within them that needed to be hidden ;
and at the moment there was indeed nothing.
After they had walked on in this way for a while
they stopped of one accord and looked round
them. They found themselves on the shore road
gazing across at Dunoon and Innellan, and they
watched for a little a paddle-steamer passing
down the estuary towards Rothesay.

" Isn't it lovely ? " said Mansie, as though
drawing her attention to a sight that had appeared just at that moment ; then, " Will we have
a rest ? "

She did not reply, but left the road and
clambered down the sloping banks of the cliff
until she reached a shelf of dry turf. Beneath
them the sea's surface ran smooth and unbroken
to the opposite shore several miles away. And
lying there they were frozen to the same immobility as the sea ; it was not a frame of flesh
and blood but a transubstantiated body that he
clasped ; for though they lay for a long time like
this they felt no lessening of their trance-like
ease, nor did his arms grow tired, so perfect was
the equilibrium that reciprocally upbore them,
an equilibrium as of a double trunk growing out
of the ground where they lay. When at last they
sat up, it was as by a single impulse coming from
without, as though a voice had called to them

both at the same moment; yet even then they could not break the spell binding them, and they remained silently leaning against each other while their eyes gazed out across the firth. Sometimes their faces turned of one accord and they kissed; the trance deepened and when they awoke it had kept that deeper darkness, and now it was a little more difficult for them to move their limbs. Only once did the spell threaten to break, letting in the menacing world. Mansie had been playing with a locket hanging at her neck; he opened it idly and saw inside a twisted strand of black hair. Something far within his mind said: " That is Tom's hair." Helen sat up and snatched it from him. " I don't want it! I don't want it!" she cried, as if in answer to an accusation he had not made, and she tore the locket from the chain and flung it into the sea. He looked at her, hardly aware yet of what she had done, but she said: " I won't have you made unhappy," and again leant towards him, closing her eyes. And while he was still wondering that she should carry about Tom's hair clasped in a locket, and still thinking of Tom's hair drowned in the sea – that gave one an uncanny feeling, as if part of Tom had been drowned without his knowing it – the spell stole over him again, the trance held them suspended, and when at last they rose and walked back the flashing arc made by the locket as it fell into the sea had been lost in the web of their dream, woven into it like the curves cut by the seagulls in their flight and the constant lines of the Highland hills opposite.

They had tea in a little tea-room on the sea front. They did not speak much; fragmentary pictures of seaweed and rocks flowed through Mansie's mind, he felt the salt scent of the sea air, and still remembered with surprise and delight Helen in her smart clothes sitting on that piece of common turf among the rough rocks and taking up a few ordinary pebbles in her hand as though it were the most natural thing in the world; and although with her fine clothes she belonged to a quite different world, calling up a vision of lace-covered sofas and curtained rooms, she had fitted perfectly into the picture and had gone splendidly with the sky and the sea and even the gritty little pebbles. Nor did the grease-spotted tablecloth in the dingy tea-room destroy the unshakable harmony between her and her sur-roundings; yet when they were out in the street again they did not take the road they had taken that afternoon, but turned their backs upon it and climbed a steep lane leading to the hill behind the town. And now as though with the closing in of the day something else which they did not know were closing in upon them, their trance became blinder, and when, reaching the top of a winding path, they saw a rowan-tree with its red berries burning in the last rays of the sun, and beyond it a field of corn transfigured in the same radiance, they looked at that strange scene as from a dark and shuttered room, and it seemed a momentary vision that must immediately vanish again. The sky darkened over them as they lay in the heather, and now they clung together until all their limbs ached. At last she rose abruptly, and as they descended the hill once more all the heaviness that had so strangely left her body during the day returned, slackening her limbs, and she leant all her weight upon his arm as though to break it.

The train was crowded, and the country lay in darkness. The other people in the carriage were weary and silent. Now and then a smile flitted across Helen's face, and her gloved hand sought his. When they walked out of the Central Station in Glasgow, the lights, after the clarity of the spaces they had left, seemed to float in a fume of dust and noise; and that acrid infusion now entered into their trance, troubling and thickening it, so that when they reached the end of the close where she lived they stood for a long time in a blind embrace which was neither happy nor sad, yet from which it seemed unendurable that they should ever be torn.

It was only when he was nearing his home that any external thought broke into Mansie's reverie. The memory of the locket falling into the sea returned very distinctly, and with it a rush of urgent anxiety for Tom. He remembered his own humiliation that evening after Isa Smith left him in the lighted tramcar. Tom must feel like that too, only far worse. It was terrible to cast off a fellow like that, terrible to cast a fellow's hair into the sea; women were hard, and he could not help blaming Helen and even feeling a little afraid of her. Yet that day had wiped off for good his humiliation with Isa Smith; it had washed everything clean again; "a clean page," the words came into his mind. But then he saw that division and atonement, wrong and right, were mingled in the love that bound Helen and him together, and this made the bond still stronger; it could never be broken. He stole softly into the house, as softly as one might steal into a place where a victim is still secretly bleeding; he hoped that Tom had not heard him, for it was very late.

5

BRAND and Ryrie had dropped in for the evening. They sat in the kitchen talking to Mansie and Jean. The table had been cleared and pushed against the wall. Brand was holding forth as usual.

" And I tell you you can't be a Christian without being a Socialist," he said, looking across at Mansie with his cold blue eyes. They were so cold that they seemed made of glass.

Mansie looked doubtful. " I don't see that," he said.

" Don't see that either," said Bob Ryrie.

" That's because you've never thought about it," Brand went on. " What did Christ say ? "

Mrs. Manson, sitting in the armchair by the fire, looked up. The tone in which Brand mentioned Christ disquieted her ; he brought out the name as he might have brought out " Smith " or " Mackay."

" What did Christ say ? That you're to love your neighbour as yourself. Is it loving your neighbour to pay him starvation wages, as lots of your churchgoing capitalists do ? As I've told

57

you before, it's the churches that have got to be converted first."

"Yes, to Socialism," said Bob Ryrie, giving Mansie a wink.

"And why not?" Jean retorted. She did not even glance at Bob Ryrie, but kept her eyes fixed on Brand.

"I thought myself that the churches were out for Christianity," said Bob, still to Mansie. "I may be mistaken of course."

Jean shrugged her shoulders.

"And so they should be," Brand seized the lead again. "That's just our quarrel with them. What have they done all these hundreds of years they've been in existence? Have they helped the weak? Have they abolished poverty? Look at the slums of Glasgow. You've never faced the problem yet. What did Christ say——"

"In 1872," said Tom sarcastically, entering in his stocking soles and going to the fireplace to get his shoes.

"Tom, Tom, my lamb, you mustna' say things like that," said Mrs. Manson, bending down to get his shoes for him or to hide her face.

Brand looked at Tom with blank uncomprehending eyes. "What did Christ say?" he repeated. "That we're all members of one another. That's what any Socialist will tell you. That's what we have been preaching for the last twenty years. And they won't see it.

And the Christians are the worst of the lot."

"Fine Christians you Socialists are!" said Tom, pulling on his shoes. "I suppose you consider Ben Tillett a Christian?"

"If he helps the weak he's a Christian."

"'Oh God, strike Lord Devonport dead'!" Tom intoned, jeeringly. "There's Christianity for you. And he gets a crowd of ignorant navvies to repeat it after him in public."

Bob Ryrie shook his head at Brand: "No, that wasn't right, you know. A fellow can go a bit too far."

Brand glanced at Jean; then he turned to Tom: "I'd like to ask you a question. Are you on Lord Devonport's side or on Ben Tillett's?"

"I'm on the side of the poor devils that are starving on account of Devonport's and Tillett's damn foolishness."

"That's all very well; but who's fighting for better pay for them, and who's fighting against it?"

"I'm for better pay all the time, but——"

"Wait a minute. What did Ben Tillett mean when he prayed to God to strike Devonport dead? Did he have any ill-will against Devonport? Not at all. He wanted to stop all these men and their families from starving. There's thousands of women and children starving because of Lord Devonport. You never think of them; you only think of him."

"Oh, you can twist anything round," said Tom, bending his red face over the shoes. "When a Socialist does a damned measly action it's bound to be right!"

"I think it was a silly thing to do," said Jean. "Besides, if you think it was right, God evidently didn't, for He didn't answer their prayer."

Tom laughed. "That's logic for you, Brand," he said. "See if you can find an answer to that." He got up and walked out, and presently the front door slammed.

Brand seemed taken aback. Then he looked across at Mansie again: "Well, as I was saying——"

6

THOUGH Jean was four years his junior, Mansie had a great respect for her opinion and felt singled out when it supported his; and so her dislike for Bob Ryrie, a dislike which nothing, it seemed, could alter, deeply disappointed him and even shook a little his own regard for his friend, although he would not admit it. After Bob's first visit to the house – it was a few weeks before Helen broke with Tom – he asked Jean a little uncertainly what she thought of Ryrie. She put her nose in the air and said: "You feel he's offering you a coupon." The blood rushed to Mansie's cheeks; it was as though he himself had been attacked, and he replied: "Bob's a gentleman! And he's the kindest-hearted fellow you'll meet."

"Well, he can keep his kindness to himself," said Jean, and it was clear that she did not consider Bob in the first class.

This was a very small class, but to her a definite one, and indeed the only one she was able to tolerate. She could not have told what qualities people had to possess to belong to it; yet she

thought in classes, and so the very first thing that
she might be expected to say when asked such a
question as Mansie's was, " He's a pure third-
rater," or " He's tenth rate." But Bob was
Mansie's best friend, and so the exasperated figure
of speech escaped her, and she felt irritated at
Mansie for forcing her to speak " in conun-
drums."

Oh, no doubt this Ryrie man was kind-hearted ;
he let you see that only too clearly ; he let you
see it in the way he shook hands, in his anxious
hopes that you might like Glasgow – as if
Glasgow belonged to him ! – in his gentlemanly
attentiveness, which made you feel that with his
eyes he was supporting you in the mere act of
living, helpfully assisting you to breathe and endure the immense strain of sitting upright in your
chair. And Jean had sat up straighter, had braced
her shoulders to hold off this smothering load
of solicitude which was about to crush her. No,
she could not stand the man, she could not stand
his brown eyes with their protective glance, nor
his brown moustache waxed at the points, which
also seemed in some way an earnest of masculine
protection, but became slightly limp, in spite of
its waxy rigidity, when the protection was blankly
ignored. She could not stand his brown tweed
suit, which recapitulated again the note of
enveloping protectiveness and gave out the
delicatest aroma of tobacco and peat, a faint,

pleasant and yet oppressive emanation of somno-
lence. She wanted to yawn, felt that she would
like to go straight to sleep, and her voice when she
replied to his polite enquiries sounded remote to
her, like a monologue heard when one is half
awake. And neither could she stand his neatly
shaven face to which the bay rum still clung like
a transparent film, making his cheeks look as
though they had been iced; nor his scrubbed
and manicured hands, nor his pipe for which he
apologised, nor the way he inclined his head, like
a servant awaiting orders. A fatuous ass, a pure
tenth-rater, she told herself, and she was angry
with Mansie for having such an acquaintance, and
angry too that she could not say so more unequivocally.

But she was quite unequivocal enough for
Mansie, and he felt both insulted in his taste and
hurt on Bob's account. For a fellow who made
people feel that he was offering them coupons
could hardly be considered first rate, and it was a
galling reflection that his best friend was not first
rate. Of course it was all a misunderstanding of
Jean's, all due to Bob's kindness of heart; and besides she hadn't seen him at his best; no, it was a
pity, but Bob hadn't been at his best. All the
same the coupon stuck, and now Mansie could
not help remembering that when he met Bob
first he too had been a trifle nonplussed, maybe a
little put off even. They had met at the Baptist

Chapel a little after Mansie's conversion. Bob
had begun to pour out information on him right
off in the helpful voice of someone directing you
to a strange address, saying, " You should go
there," or " You should join them, a nice set of
fellows." Mansie had felt quite rushed. Yes, it
seemed impossible for Bob to say anything at all
without making you think that he was lending
you a helping hand; even when he told a funny
story he seemed to be making you a present of it,
so that you might win social credit for yourself
by telling it to someone else; well, perhaps a
fellow who was so genuinely anxious to help as
Bob got into the habit of talking in that way and
just couldn't help it. But later Mansie had
stopped thinking about it, and especially after
Bob had taken him to that church soirée where
all those Boy Scouts were. For they were exactly
the same, all eager to help; he couldn't make
them out at first, thought they were dashed
forward; but then he saw it was all quite
genuine: when you lived in a big place like
Glasgow you had to be on the look-out for
opportunities to help people, that is if you had any
decency in you at all; you might need a helping
hand some time yourself. Jean didn't realise that
yet; she was new to Glasgow and didn't know
how hard life might be for a girl there, not to
speak of temptations. He didn't care whether
Bob was first rate according to her silly notions

or not. She could dash well think what she liked.

But in the ensuing months Jean showed no sign of getting over her aversion; it became more frank, and so it was no wonder if Bob didn't do himself justice; he hadn't a dog's chance. All the same he was a dashed sight too anxious. After all, had he any need to go to such pains to please Jean? He actually seemed to be quite put out because Jean didn't take to him, and he couldn't help trying again, getting more and more red in the face every time; no, he didn't show to advantage then.

Nevertheless when one evening after Bob had left Jean turned to Mansie and said: "I object to people making eyes at me because I'm your cousin," Mansie flared up and shouted, "He's too dashed good for you!" He had had no intention of saying such a thing; it just jumped out, and for a moment he felt quite taken aback.

"Well, you'd better tell him so," replied Jean. "He bores me stiff."

"Everybody else in the house gets on with Bob. Why shouldn't you?"

"He doesn't make eyes at them."

"You flatter yourself if you fancy he's making eyes at you!" Mansie became angry again. "He's only trying to be humanly decent."

"I prefer people to keep their distance."

There was no use talking to her, that was

clear, and when a few evenings later Bob said
with a slight catch in his voice, " Mansie, I'm
afraid I'm making no headway with your cousin ;
I've done my best to be nice to her, but it's no
use," Mansie replied, " Don't you bother, Bob.
You've been too dashed considerate to her. Yes,
by gum ! " But then he suddenly felt embarrassed ; they walked on without looking at each
other ; and when Bob broke the silence it was to
speak of something quite different.

After this Bob was careful to treat Jean with
distant politeness, and the change in fact seemed
to take her somewhat aback. Mansie decided
that Bob had got the better of the exchanges
after all ; but that was nothing to be surprised
at, for Bob could be quite the man of the world
when he chose to take the trouble. And Bob's
superiority remained unchallenged until David
Brand appeared. By bad luck Bob happened to
drop in that evening after Brand had been holding
forth for more than an hour, and the sight of
Jean sitting listening with her eyes on Brand's
face seemed to knock him flat. He began to talk
to her in his old confidential tone ; she stared at
him in surprise for a moment and then snubbed
him ; but he was completely rattled and couldn't
stop until he had been snubbed three or four
times. Then he got into an argument with
Brand about Socialism ; but Brand just played
with him, giving Jean a look every now and then ;

and at last Bob simply turned tail and had to console himself with a long and helpful talk with Mansie in the lobby. Mansie had never seen Bob at such a disadvantage, and was sorry he had ever invited Brand to the house.

He couldn't understand what Jean saw in Brand anyway. A striking-looking fellow, no doubt about it, with his Roman nose and his yellow hair; but there was something queer and cold about him; you could never think of him as a friend. Mansie had met him first at a Y.M.C.A. dance. It was in the men's cloakroom, Mansie was standing before the looking-glass putting the finishing touches to his necktie, and some fellows were discussing the Insurance Act. "What do you say to that, Brand?" someone had asked. Mansie turned round at that moment, and he saw a tall, lanky young man raising his head, which had been bowed over a dancing-pump that he was pulling on. "I think it's claptrap," came the reply in a falsetto voice, but Mansie was so astonished by the beauty of the briefly upturned face, which was now bent over the other pump, that he continued to stare in a trance at the smooth flaxen hair presented object-tively to him, its fairness and the even masses in which it lay reminding him somehow of butter. Afterwards he saw Brand dancing; he was a very bad dancer and seemed to talk to his partners all the time. It was not until near the end of the dance that Brand strolled up, stood beside him, and made some remark about the heat. "Lots of nice girls here," Mansie said, not knowing what else to say; but Brand replied, "I'm not interested in females, I'm here to make converts." Females! thought Mansie, so it must have been Socialism that he was spouting to them! and as a new dance was just beginning he rushed away.

But next Sunday afternoon at the Y.M.C.A. Brand fastened on to him, seemed in fact to have taken quite a fancy to him, and although Mansie didn't really care much for the fellow, no doubt about it he was a dashed handsome figure to be seen with. But though Brand was a brilliant success in the Church Literary Society, he didn't make a really deep impression on Mansie until that evening in late spring when they went to see *Arms and the Man*. And it wasn't because Brand laughed at all the right places, looking round him contemptuously, that Mansie was impressed; what struck him was a sentence that Brand dropped carelessly as they were walking to the tramcar; he said, "I think I'll have to write a play too." Then Mansie realised all at once that Brand lived in a completely different world from him. For to Mansie the writing of a book or play, even one he could understand, was a mysterious act, he simply didn't understand how it was done; and yet here was a fellow who

after being at a play one could make neither
head nor tail of simply said : " I'll have to write
a play too ! " Mansie felt excited, yet was
resolved not to show it, but to reply in the same
tone. " You should, Brand," he said. " I
think you really should."

Brand was in fact very handsome, and that was
probably enough to give Jean an immediate
respect for him ; but what won her final approval
was the fact that he carried his handsome looks
almost scornfully, as though he ignored them ;
for that seemed to her the perfection of good
taste. And so it might have been had he merely
ignored them, magnanimously declining to em-
ploy them to his advantage ; but it would be
nearer the truth to say that he was completely
oblivious of them, and that they were thrown
away on him and so bereft of all meaning. They
were like a thankless gift that he was always
trying to forget, that he even did his best to
deface ; for he had so little respect for his
exquisite features that he was continually knit-
ting his brow like a schoolboy and twisting his
mouth into peevish lines that deserved to look
mean, and would have done so in any face less
perfectly formed. When he did this, such
treatment of a rare physical miracle gave one a
sense of ingratitude, even of desecration ; nevertheless it was ineffectual, for no matter how he
scowled, the lines instead of disfiguring his face

merely fell effortlessly into new patterns of symmetry, one more interesting than the other. No, he could not escape from the beauty that had been so unwelcomely thrust upon him.

But though he could not rid himself of it he could refuse to impregnate it with life. So his face was like the photographed faces of actors which seem to be mutely begging for a rôle to bring them to life and add expression and character, no matter of what tinge, to those unemployed features with their tell-tale vacancy. And Brand's face sometimes struck one as that of a man waiting for his rôle, a rôle that should have been his life, a rôle that he would never find. His talk, too, was as trite as that of actors or popular preachers who after declaiming as though in another world, " I am dying, Egypt, dying," or " Ho ! every one that thirsteth, come ye to the waters " have nothing left to utter in private but the stale clichés of political and social snobbery. It shocks one that they should do so with such flat conviction. But what shocks one still more is the recognition that after all they are merely acting another part, an innate and compulsory part which has no connection whatever with Antony or Hamlet or Othello, with Christ or Paul. The conversation of Brand seemed to belong to a part such as this, a part which did not suit him, which was false and even badly played, and yet had been imposed upon him so imperatively that he would

have to act it all his life. But his words had also
the sonorous emptiness that is so often found in
the conversation of men who spend their lives
advertising commodities which they have not
made and will never use, but who nevertheless
become mechanically rapturous upon the virtues
of those commodities whenever a prospective
buyer comes in sight. It had that false and
portentously edifying conviction ; but also, somewhat incongruously, a touch of the flat assurance
of a school-teacher imparting to his class information that means hardly anything to him ; securely
supported in a sense of right when he asserts that
Milton is the greatest English poet after Shake-
speare (although Milton bores him), or that man's
chief end is to glorify God (although he has never
in his life felt the slightest impulse to glorify God).
And Brand was a school-teacher.

So it was only in their form that Brand's
opinions differed from those of a gentlemanly
actor or an unctuous business man. He had been
brought up in a Socialist family ; his father was
an atheistic Marxian ; and only when he was
twenty-five did David discover Christianity. The
discovery was so novel that the ideas he encountered seemed novel too, not unlike those of Ibsen
and Shaw, and in his mind Christ was enthroned
between those two contemporary idols as a great
advanced thinker ; a position which, Brand was
really convinced in his heart, conferred fresh glory

on the New Comer, though he was fond of saying – to impress people with his brilliance – that Jesus was the most advanced and revolutionary of them all. Yet he felt that he had done Jesus a favour in promoting Him to such company, and so he spoke of Him with involuntary condescension; but then he spoke of everything with involuntary condescension – it may have been because he spent so much of his time in teaching. And besides, the people he had to teach now were Christians, and they simply did not know the rudiments of their own subject! So he had to make the matter as simple as possible.

Yet it may be that he could not help making it simple; for a man who has to simplify knowledge for several hours a day to suit minds of twelve or thirteen often ends by simplifying everything; he may acquire such a love for simplification that only simplified ideas give him pleasure. And in fact the more elementary a truth was the more pleasure Brand found in uttering it; and if he could impart to it a sort of flashing triteness he himself was dazzled, as though he had achieved an epigram. So when he came across the axiom, " God is love," it was not the statement itself that thrilled him, but the tellingly terse form in which it was couched; and he did not see anything blasphemous in this treatment of a saying which all the wisdom of the world is insufficient to comprehend. For a school-teacher of the conventional kind may not only admire simplified statements ; he is capable of falling in love with them simply as statements. He falls in love with them as the commercial traveller falls in love with gypsum, clinkers, or asbestos jointing ; for though he can make no more personal use of them than the commercial traveller of those wares, yet they are the things that give meaning to his deliberate and rational activity as a human being. But his love is less humble and passionate than the love of a commercial traveller for asbestos jointing ; for he has a monopoly of his goods and the commercial traveller has not, and he can pass them on to the recipient without being obliged to exercise the arts of persuasion, whereas his commercial brother has to summon all his eloquence, has to plead, to propitiate, to dazzle. So when Brand made any simple assertion which his interlocutor refused to accept on the spot, he had a habit of saying : " I'm telling you." After asserting that Jesus was a Socialist or that the Kingdom of Heaven was within you – if you voted intelligently – he would add, " I'm telling you," and it may be that, yielding to habit, he once or twice capped even the sublime axiom, " God is love," with this unseemly addition. For he could not utter even that saying without seeming to clinch something, without appearing to be making a point.

All this, however, is only the outside of Brand,

and what lay behind it would be hard to say. It is questionable indeed, whether anything lay behind, for the thing one was most vividly aware of was a want. And in that want there must of necessity have been some deficiency of sex. Nothing else could have made him such a glittering and vacant fool; for even a hardened libertine, if his attention were seriously drawn to the sentence, " God is love," would see at least that it was a very extraordinary statement, even if he did not understand it. But to Brand it was not in any way extraordinary; it was an obvious truth contained in a simple sentence of three words. So his lanky body with its unselfconscious and yet ungainly movements was that of one unaware of life; his bones beneath the clothes of a tall man were the shameless, raw bones of a boy of twelve or thirteen. He had also the shy affectionateness of a boy; but he had no charity, for charity is an adult virtue. And catching sight of his inarticulate limbs stretched out like a cry for help as he half lay in a chair, one saw all at once that his words were not after all those of an actor or a teacher, but those of a bright boy of twelve, and one forgave him and felt sorry for him, no matter how intolerable his arrogance may have been a moment before.

It was probably his sexlessness that attracted Jean. Had she known it was sexlessness, it is true, she would have been repelled. But being herself passionate and yet self-repressed, she saw in Brand's demeanour only a scornful superiority to the fatuity of desire. She hated sentiment, she hated the disorder and disingenuousness of love, she hated, above all, women who got left with illegitimate children; she hated them with the naïve hatred of one who passionately disliked ambiguity. So Brand's logical advocacy of women's suffrage and common-sense exposition of religion appealed equally to her; they seemed to exclude all sentimentality. She began to go to women's suffrage meetings with Brand, then to plays, then to Socialist demonstrations. He never touched her or treated her like a woman, and she felt that she had come at last to know a rational being. Nobody else in the house liked Brand, and perhaps that made her go about more constantly with him than she would otherwise have done. It also made her oblivious of the strange state Tom was in.

7

A MAN who has desperately fought for the possession of an unattainable object finds himself in a very strange position when he realises that it is worthless and that his desire for it has suddenly vanished. Then it may appear to him that he should be perfectly happy again; for the cause of his suffering is removed, and the things that once gave him pleasure are still to be had; he has only to stretch out his hand for them. The sun still shines; friends, music-halls, saw-dusted pubs, the lights and crowds of the city, the excitements of football and wrestling – all these exist unaffected by the experience he has passed through. Everything seems to be as it was before; yet something has changed: a hole has yawned in his world, and through it all the warmth that used to be in things has drained away, leaving them cold and empty. He feels the heat of the sun on his face and the backs of his hands, but it is stopped there as by an icy casing; it does not warm his limbs. He breathes the sharp autumnal air, but it is thin and bodiless, an invisible empty something that he draws into his lungs ; and although there is no danger of its failing him and he inhales it automatically, yet he finds that breathing requires a slight effort, an effort that tires him, for it is meaningless. His friends too have become curiously external and objective, have receded into a different dimension like figures in a painting, and for the first time he notices lines in their faces that he had never noticed before, lines which, if he were not outside the picture himself, might make him dislike those people. Nor do the jokes of music-hall comedians give him pleasure, for all that he can see in them is a mechanism for producing the automatic spasm of laughter ; he sees this clearly, although he is far less capable of analysing his impressions than many of the people who laugh. Sometimes in the midst of wrestling he suddenly surrenders to his opponent's grip where he could have jerked himself free ; for the knowledge that the stronger must inevitably overcome the weaker makes all resistance meaningless, and his mind refuses to strike out the sudden inspiration that would extricate him, for that too seems irrelevant. And the feeling that nothing is involved but two fixed units of animal energy, incarnated ludicrously in two sweating bodies, disgusts him, and he stops going to the club.

Seeing that so many things are empty, although still perplexingly palpable to his eyes and mind, he falls back on the most simple and gross and therefore dependable realities in his life: on necessity and deliberate pleasure. He rises every morning to go to work, because he must; and he drinks, because drink, if taken in sufficient quantities, can be relied upon to produce an effect as independent of the unstable human will as a natural law. So he clings to drink as the one solid thing in a world that has become insubstantial. Yet he does not drink to forget, but simply to comfort himself: to fill the vacuum within him with a warm and friendly presence, with something that will lie down and coil itself snugly inside him like an affectionate, sleek, soft animal, say a little black puppy. He feels then so intimately united with a cordial and caressing presence that he prefers to sit alone over his beer or his whisky, so that nothing so incalculable as human society may interfere with his pleasure.

But the fact that he has become a solitary drinker shows that other things besides the things he sees and hears have gone empty and blind: his ideas, his very actions. His actions have lost their content, have become neutral, so that now he does without scruple things of which once he would have been ashamed even to think. So when one evening Tom Manson, while sitting before the fire in the empty kitchen, caught sight of his mother's purse on the mantelpiece and got up and looked inside it, he did so casually and

absently, as one turns over an illustrated paper in
a doctor's waiting-room. And when, seeing a
number of coins inside, he took one out and put
it in his pocket, it was a self-evident and yet
unimportant action, the mere shifting of an
object from one place to another. He felt
neither guilty nor elated, he hardly felt interested,
and the fact that presently he put on his shoes and
went out to the pub at the corner of the street
was only an accidental effect of his original
action – if it could be called an action – and not
the proof of any design. When he had drunk the
half-crown he felt warmed and comforted, but
that was all ; the coin was gone, and it had such
an indirect relation to the glow he felt within
him that it might never have existed at all, far
less have been stolen by him two hours before ;
he scarcely gave the matter a thought. Had he
kept the half-crown, or had he spent only part
of it, no doubt his conscience would have
smitten him every time he heard the jingle in his
pockets ; but the half-crown was gone, and by
next evening the effect was gone too. Yet when
next evening his mother complained that she
must have lost a two-shilling piece he said to her :
" You should be more careful with your money ;
you leave it lying about too much " ; and he
meant what he said. And on Saturday he gave
her an extra five shillings for his weekly board :
" Got a bonus this week," he said.

But Mrs. Manson continued to leave her purse lying about, until one day she discovered that a pound note was missing. That was a serious matter; she could not get over it, and her lamentations drove Tom into a fury. "It serves you right!" he shouted. "Can't you look after your money?" And on Saturday he did not give her anything extra; it was her own fault, and he needed all his money for himself. After that the purse was not left lying about.

Yet the thought that Tom might have stolen the money never entered Mrs. Manson's head; she could not imagine anyone she knew doing such a thing; and when she read in the newspapers of thefts what she saw was the stylised image of a thief, a being so different from the people she knew that had she interrogated her imagination she would probably have found him furnished with a distinctive cut of clothes, a subtle and inconspicuous livery. So she never suspected Tom, although Mansie was continually complaining of his thefts. Now it would be Mansie's ivory-headed stick that was missing, now one of his ties; he would find it next morning crumpled up and flung on the floor of Tom's room. The fellow might at least take care of one's things, if he insisted on pinching them! Mansie suffered in silence for a while, and when at last he complained to Jean and Mrs. Manson, Jean remained silent and Mrs. Manson said quite unexpectedly : " I never thought you twa boys wad be enemies." That silenced Mansie, and he could not complain to Tom either, for they were not on speaking terms ; and besides, in the midst of his anger sometimes he felt strangely touched by those naïve thefts ; they were so childish, they were what a little boy might do to an elder brother who did not love him. Occasionally he was actually alarmed at Tom's familiar use of his things ; it touched one so intimately, it was like a threat, and it was unnatural too, quite unlike Tom ; and the thought would come into his mind : Tom must be very unhappy. But then his exasperation, tinged with a little dread, would return again, and seeing that his mother and Jean refused to do anything he spoke bitterly of his wrongs to Helen.

Tom's own feelings when he took Mansie's ties and vests might have been expressed in the words : " Why should he have everything ? " and although he was not consciously aware of Helen as an item in that everything, no doubt it was she, and she alone, that was at the back of his mind. So his open use of his brother's belongings was not merely a silent announcement that Mansie was outside the pale now, with no right to protest, whatever was done to him ; it was also the symbolical declaration of a claim to have unconditionally all that Mansie had, and Mansie had been wise in seeing a threat in it. A very indeterminate and quite powerless threat, however, almost a fictitious one, for the Helen that Tom wanted was not the Helen who had passed into Mansie's possession, but an illusion, once cherished and now dead, which his brother was powerless to restore to him. He did not know what he wanted from Mansie, and so he took whatever he could get.

8

ONE EVENING Mansie decided to walk home instead of taking the tramcar as usual. He had been in the office all day giving an account of his last quarter's work and going over the possibilities of opening up new custom during the coming weeks; the manager had been very pleased with his report, but Mansie felt cramped and a little stifled after sitting all day in the poky office – the manager had actually insisted on sending out for dinner – and now he wanted to stretch his legs. And besides he was curious to find out how Eglinton Street would strike him now after such a long time, for passing through it in the tramcar every evening was quite a different thing from walking from end to end of it on foot. Months and months it must have been since he had done that; not more than once or twice since he had been taken from the office and put on the road. What could have possessed him to walk home through that street every evening during those first months in Glasgow? Of course, it was Bob Ryrie; Bob had told him that he must take exercise for the sake of his health. All the same Eglinton Street was a queer place to take exercise in ; not much health to be picked up in Eglinton Street. It had made him feel quite low-spirited at times, especially when he was tired. Well, he got enough movement now as it was without having to walk through Eglinton Street.

He crossed the Jamaica Bridge. Dusk was falling and the lamps were being lit ; they ran in two straight rows up the slightly rising street, and those in the distance hung in a soft moony haze that was almost fairy-like. The pavement was damp and sticky, though there had been no rain, and now it seemed to him that it had always been like that. After passing through on the tramcar, too, one felt uncomfortably near the ground down here, as though walking along the bottom of a gully which was always slightly damp, while a little above the level of one's head ran a smooth and clean high road. When a tramcar sailed by with all its lights on he felt tempted to run after it.

Astonishing the number of dirty squalling children that were down here, down here the whole time by all appearances, for you never saw them anywhere else, perhaps they never got up at all, poor little beggars. And the way they yelled and screamed was enough to scare you ; wasn't like a human sound at all. Yet you never heard them when you were passing on the tramcar. And

into Mansie's mind came a phrase that the
Reverend John had been fond of using, a
phrase from the Bible : " Crying to the heavens."
Perhaps that was what the poor little beggars
were trying to do, their voices sounded so desperate ; but their cries remained down here, all the
the same, seemed in a way to belong to this level,
perhaps never got as far even as the house roofs,
seeing that you never heard them in the tramcar.
A terrible life for those youngsters. And the
girls in shawls ; walked straight at you, made you
step out of their way pretty quick, and even then
brushed against you intentionally as if to say :
If you walk here you've got to take the conse-
quences. And you never saw them speaking to
these poor little kids, not even speaking to them.
Wouldn't like Helen to have to walk through this
street, by gum ! A difference between this and
that shore road outside Gourock.

Maybe it would be best to take the tramcar at
the next stop after all. He hesitated, but to stand
down here frightened one ; walking was bad
enough, but standing was far worse ; and so
before he had time to weigh the matter he abruptly
went on again, and as he did so he felt angry. A
fine kind of street to be in a Christian town !
Blatchford was quite right, by gum ; streets like
this had no right to exist, people could say what
they liked. A warm cloud of stench floated into
his face, he hurried past a fish-and-chip shop, and

in a flash Eglinton Street rose before him from
end to end as something complete, solid and
everlasting ; it had been there all the time, he
realised, and it would always be there, something
you had to walk round every morning and
evening, that forced you to go out of your way
until at last you got used to your new road and
it seemed the natural one. As he passed the shop,
whose crumbling door-posts seemed rotted and
oozing with rancid grease, something made him
glance up. Yes, there in the next close mouth
she was standing, the great fat red-haired woman
with her arms clasped about her overflowing
breasts as if to keep them from escaping. Queer,
he had clean forgotten her. But there she was,
and it seemed to him that she too had been there
all the time, standing at the end of the close and
keeping them from escaping ; and she too was
something that one had to walk round, a fixed
obstacle that could never be removed. He
hurried on. Terrible to have to live down here ;
but the street was mounting, the houses were
thinning, the crowds were thinning too, only a
few had managed to struggle up here where he
was ; and they were better dressed, they were
like himself, they lived in the suburbs. And his
confidence began to return, and with it pity for
those poor beggars who were shaken together
down there to the bottom of the street like rubbish
at the bottom of a sack. A church. Queer to see

a church here. A group of young men, clean-
shaven and with mufflers round their necks, stood
bristling on the pavement and stared at him without moving aside. He stepped into the street –
still muddier, still nearer the ground down here –
and made to walk round them ; but then he
changed his mind – these fellows had to be taught
a lesson ! – and so he strode straight across to the
tramcar halt at the other side of the street and
stopped there as though waiting. He wouldn't
give them the satisfaction of thinking he had
stepped off the pavement for them !

But he had to wait a long time, for all the
tramcars were full. Now and then he glanced
across at the bristling group on the other pavement ; it was almost dark now, but they were
standing under a lamp-post and he could see them
quite clearly. The stream of home-going pedes-
trians flowed more thickly now along the pavement, but where the group was stationed it
made a bend, wavered, turned aside, and then
flowed on again. Mansie's anger mounted and
mounted. A set of hooligans ! And the sight
of that long, living, helpless animal stretching
away under the rows of lamps until it was lost in
a dirty haze, stretching so far that it seemed tired
and weighed down by its own dragging length,
but yet flowed laboriously round this small hard
obstacle when it came to it, made him far angrier
than his own discomfiture had done. Tom

wouldn't let himself be shouldered aside like that, by gum he wouldn't! He would teach those young hooligans a lesson; he would send them flying! And Mansie longed for Tom to appear, and when at last he got on to a tram in which there was only standing room he blamed the roughs for that too, and his anger flamed up again. *They* flourished in the slums, those hooligans, it suited them down to the ground, they were in clover. It was time to put an end to these plague spots; for that was what they were, just plague spots. But those other poor beggars at the bottom of the street, it was no joke for them; a fellow couldn't close his eyes to the fact; they were a problem. Blatchford might be an atheist, but he was quite right there, people could say what they liked. The words of Gibson in the office came into his mind: " And what about the poor bloody little children? " but he did not smile this time; Gibson was a bit of a card, and an extremist too, but by gum he was right. It was enough to make a fellow join the Clarion Scouts. And as he got off the tramcar at the corner of his street he half wished that it was Brand he had to meet that evening, instead of Bob Ryrie.

9

IN A HOUSEHOLD consisting of four people a state of armed silence between two of them is like the opening of a hole in the middle of the floor. They have all moved about at their ease, they have sat where they liked; but now their chairs are pushed back against the wall and when they speak to each other it is across a gulf. Arithmetically the silence between Tom and Mansie should have affected only themselves, and the possibilities of intercourse that remained were obviously considerable. Mrs. Manson and Jean could still speak to everyone in the house, and Tom and Mansie could each speak to Mrs. Manson and Jean. But though it was on this strictly arithmetical foundation that the new domestic arrangements were based, for there was nothing else to base them on, the subtler effects of the silence were inescapable. One of these was irremediably to reduce the size of the family. When both Tom and Mansie were in no one could talk naturally, and so they were always wishing one of their number away. For then the family was reborn again; a family, it was true, that had been lopped, and suffered from an unuttered bereavement; yet nothing unites a household more selfishly and tenderly than the absence of one of its members. And if Mansie and Tom, the inconstant links in that constant chain – by turns the bereaved and the absent – felt their position an equivocal one, that only made them identify themselves more eagerly with the family while the chance was given them. They did so as if under the approaching shadow of extinction, as if they were taking a last chance.

Or at least it was so at the beginning, before the new state of things had hardened and been accepted with the selfishness of habit. Then Tom, already careless of himself, very soon became careless too of what his mother and Jean thought of him, and began to use the house as a mere convenience. It was Mrs. Manson who suffered most, for Jean and Mansie were very often out during the evenings. But even when Jean was in talk was as constrained now in Tom's presence as it had once been when both he and Mansie were there. For by some mysterious legerdemain Tom seemed to evoke by himself, as he sat morosely over the fire, that gulf in the middle of the floor which they both wanted to forget.

And Tom was in the house a great deal. His weekly routine had become so mechanical that it could be calculated beforehand. By Tuesday night he had drunk all his wages, except for the few shillings to take him to and from his work, and from Tuesday to Friday he sat over the fire every evening, staring into the coals and doing nothing, yet bitterly annoyed if he was interrupted in that empty occupation. He seemed to find a peculiar satisfaction in the warmth and silence, a satisfaction without pleasure, however; indeed a strictly impersonal satisfaction. For it was not himself that he warmed there, but his grudge against Mansie and Helen, and as this was a private duty rather than a pleasure it was only natural that his expression should be austere and jealously guarded. Sometimes, partly out of old habit, partly out of joyless self-indulgence, he took out his long cherished dreams of a free life in the colonies and warmed them there too. But by now they had become as cold and empty as everything else; they were like pictures hung up on the wall and shuttered in with glass; and even when he thought of ships, often all that would come into his mind was the neat little model of a liner high and dry in its glass case in the window of a shipping agency in Renfield Street. All this was no longer a possibility in his mind, hardly even a dream, simply a picture; yet he took pleasure in contemplating that picture with his mother sitting so near him quite unaware of what he was doing; it was a malicious, almost a revengeful pleasure.

The family had to make a show of unity when
anyone came in, but that was quite easy, and the
insincerity it involved was actually enjoyable ;
for when one after another the whole family had
spoken or replied to the visitor, the invisible gulf
seemed to close ; it became a merely private
abyss that existed only while no spectator was
there to see it. They all felt this particularly
when Bob Ryrie called ; but Brand, being
absorbed in himself, left them in their isolation ;
and besides Tom was always quarrelling with him.
It was partly Brand himself that he disliked,
partly Brand's ideas ; and when Brand brought
out as a last appeal, " You must give the bottom
dog a chance," Tom would retort, " You can
say what you like, but there'll always be wasters,
and why should decent chaps have to pay for
their damn foolishness ? They've too damn
much done for them as it is." And the fact that
Mansie was coming more and more to agree
that the bottom dog must be given a chance
winged Tom's anger ; such sentiments in Mansie
seemed the most open and shameless hypocrisy.

Jean, to Brand's surprise, always took Tom's
side in those arguments. It was partly an indirect demonstration that she considered Tom
ill-used, partly an act of loyalty to the family.
And when she joined the I.L.P. she told Brand
that Tom must not know about it. But such
things cannot be hid ; Tom soon came to know,

and, although he did not reproach her, he felt
that she had betrayed him, and he no longer
argued with Brand, but simply ignored him.
Mrs. Manson too was hurt by Jean's action, and
it was only when Mansie as well as Brand assured
her that Socialism was Christianity in practice,
and that the Reverend John himself was coming
more and more round to it, that she was content
to be uneasily reassured.

Nevertheless Jean's action was to her only
another proof of the corrupting influence of
Glasgow. In her heart she blamed Glasgow for
all the misfortunes that had happened since they
had come south, though she did not say this for
fear of being laughed at. Yet it was inconceivable
to her that had they all stayed in the surroundings
she knew and trusted, Mansie should have taken
Tom's girl. It was simply the portion of the
corruption of Glasgow allotted to them, their
private share of the corruption that was visible
in the troubled, dirty atmosphere, the filth and
confusion of the streets, the cynical frankness,
hitherto unknown to her, with which people
here talked of their privatest affairs, their fathers
and mothers, sisters and brothers. She could
not understand them or their ways, and she grew
shy of talking about Tom and Mansie even to
Jean, and especially after Jean joined the I.L.P.
For with that Jean had identified herself with
Glasgow; she had become by deliberate choice

a Glasgow girl, and – who could tell ? – perhaps she would no longer even understand. And when one evening Mrs. Manson found Robert Blatchford's *Britain for the British* in a drawer in Mansie's bedroom, it seemed to her that she no longer understood her family and that Glasgow had taken them and made them almost as strange as itself.

But worse was her fear of all the machinery, machinery she did not understand, and with which Tom was so unavoidably associated. Indeed Tom had now more accidents than ever ; his hands were perpetually in bandages. He had always been reckless ; he was now indifferent as well ; but what exposed him most of all to accidents was the fact that, feeling shut out from everything, he felt shut out too from the very work he was doing every day, and so never penetrated within it to that security which work itself seems to give. He never reached that almost trance-like abstraction which we envy in the workman bowed over his bench, enclosed in his task as in a private Eden where time no longer exists, so remote and calm that even a child will become quiet and hesitate to speak to him. Tom remained outside, and this made him irritated with his tools, and in his irritation he began to treat them disrespectfully, began indeed to acquire an impatient scorn for machinery wherever he encountered it. Nothing, however, punishes

disrespect more promptly and ruthlessly than
machinery, and when Tom was brought home
late one Saturday night with his head bandaged
and his blue serge suit covered with mud, it was
because he had treated a tramcar with insufficient
deference. He had been drinking; yet while
descending the stairs to get off he had provoca-
tively kept one hand in his trouser pocket, using
only the other as a support. When, after what
seemed to him a long time, he found himself
lying in dirt and water in the street with a crowd
of strange people round him, he naturally enough
felt cold and miserable, for it was the middle of
November; but he also felt a little frightened.
These people standing round meant well, he
could see that; yet he was helplessly exposed to
them like an exhibit, and the overpowering stream
of kindness that they poured down on him was
like a threat and filled him with sudden panic;
he felt as though he had been lynched in some
strange way, lovingly and tenderly lynched by the
assembled Y.M.C.A. So that he was glad when
a young man raised him up, asked his address
and led him home. Someone had bound up his
head, which felt stiff, tight and wooden, and it
was with surprise that he felt under the bandage a
quite soft, pulsing trickle.

Next day was Sunday. Sunday morning was
always a bad time for him, and he lay in bed
gloomily listening to the church bells jangling;

there were loud pompous peals with blank intervals which filled him with apprehension, and busy fretful nagging little bells that went on and on ; it was like a tin factory gone mad. His head throbbed, and when he rose to draw up the blinds he felt so queer that he walked over to the mirror instead.   Christ ! he was looking bad with that bandage on his head and the black rings round his eyes ; he looked a real waster. And he went back to bed again without troubling even to pull up the blinds : a real waster, and he would never be anything else.

He refused to see a doctor, although for several days his head hummed and rang, and at the back, where the wound was, there clung a lump of pain ; it felt like a clod of hardened mud that would not be dislodged. At last the pain went away and his scalp healed. And in spite of his indifference, his relief was so great that he resolved to pull himself together and go straight.

When Mansie first heard of Tom's accident he was very angry. A fine way to behave, the fool would break his neck some time yet ! But when Tom began to go straight, keeping decent company, dressing neatly and taking a drink only now and then, Mansie became ashamed of his annoyance. He expected every day that Tom would suddenly turn to him and say something, for the fellow was completely changed, he had quite a different look about him ; and when Tom

gave no sign of speaking Mansie felt a little hurt.
But on one account he was sincerely relieved by
Tom's reformation; for now he felt there was
nothing to prevent his joining the Clarion Scouts.
With a brother who was a waster he would never
have been quite sure; it might have looked a bit
fishy, for lots of people looked upon Socialism
as fishy. Pure prejudice, of course; the crowds
he had met at Socialist demonstrations were a
very decent lot; welcomed you too, no side
about them, a friendly set of fellows. So Mansie
decided to take the plunge; with Bob joining at
the same time one felt better about it. And once
his application form was filled in and sent off a
surprise awaited him; it was as though the
Masonic circle of decent fellows had widened
infinitely all at once, and he felt as a visionary
democrat feels when he sees everywhere hosts of
free and intelligent electors spring up at some
great extension of the franchise, hosts of free and
intelligent electors where before there had been
a dull and slavish mass. The very distinguishing
marks of decent fellows were radically altered,
the old marks seemed inessential and ridiculous,
and it was almost by a whole world of decent
fellows that Mansie now delightedly saw himself
surrounded. You had only to look below the
surface, and even those hooligans in Eglinton
Street might turn out to be much better than they
seemed.

PART TWO

10

THE PROCESSION was gathering in George Square. It was a warm still May morning; a few white clouds floated far up in the sky. As Mansie turned the corner of St. Vincent Street he saw, far away, the banners languidly waving in the square, waving in silence, for no sound came from those parti-coloured rectangular blocks of human beings, which from here looked as peaceful and dumb as the rectangular buildings frowning above them. Mansie's footsteps rang sharply in the deserted street. It was the first Sunday in May.

As he drew nearer, and on the motionless rectangles isolated points of movement started out and spread into an imperceptible ripple running along the whole line, he wished that Bob Ryrie had not had to call off at the last moment ; but a fellow could not take risks with a bad cold. At last he reached the procession and paused on the pavement, feeling very exposed while he looked around him distractedly for some face he knew. A voice quite near at hand shouted his name ; it was like a lifeline thrown out to

him where he was standing on the pavement.
Why, there were the Clarion Scouts almost under
his nose, and he hadn't seen them! He smiled
back and hastily fell in at the rear beside a
white-faced pot-bellied man whom he did not
know.

And immediately he was enclosed in peace. It
was as though he had stepped out of a confused
and distracted zone into calm and safety, as
though the procession had protectively enfolded
him, lifted him up and set him down again on
the farther bank of a tranquil river among this
multitude who like him had reached the favoured
land; and the people who passed on the pavement with averted or hostile or curious eyes, on
their way to church or merely out for a walk,
had no longer any power over him; for they
were still wandering out there in exile, out
there on the pavement, and he was safe, at
home and free. Yet one thing still troubled
him: that he was in the last line of the procession, so that the threatening world yawned
at his very heels; but when a new contingent
from the Kingston I.L.P. marched up and
stationed itself behind him his security became
perfect; he was embedded in fold after fold of
security.

So that now he had leisure to look round. A
little in front of him a bareheaded man in a brown
velvet jacket and knickerbockers was carrying a

child on his shoulder. It was a little girl, and
when she turned her head to look down on all
those strange faces her yellow hair glinted in the
sun. Mansie could not take his eyes from her,
and when the procession began to move, when,
in a long line like the powerful and easy rise and
fall of a quiet surge, the ranked shoulders in
front of him swung up and down, bearing forward on their surface that gay and fragile little
bark, unexpected tears rose into Mansie's throat.
But when presently from the front of the procession the strains of the " Marseillaise " rolled
back towards him over the surface of that quietly
rising and falling sea, gathering force as it came
until at last it broke round him in a stationary
storm of sound in which his own voice was
released, he no longer felt that the little girl
riding on the shoulder of the surge was more
beautiful than anything else, for everything was
transfigured : the statues in George Square
standing in the sky and fraternally watching them,
the vacant buildings, the empty warehouses which
they passed when presently they turned into
Glassford Street, the rising and falling shoulders,
even the pot-bellied, middle-aged man by his
side ; for all distinction had been lost, all
substance transmuted in this transmutation of
everything into rhythmical motion and sound.
He was not now an isolated human being walking
with other isolated human beings from a definite

place to a definite place, but part of a perfect
rhythm which had arisen, he did not know how ;
and as that rhythm deepened, so that all sense of
effort vanished in it, he no longer seemed even to
be propelled by his own will but rather to be
floating, and with him all those people in front
and behind : the whole procession seemed to be
calmly floating down a sunny river flanked with
rocky cliffs on either side, floating like a long
wooded island where the trees stand in orderly
ranks and breathe out fragrance and coolness to
either shore. His arms and shoulders sprouted
like a tree, scents of spring filled his nostrils,
and when, still gazing in a trance at the bareheaded man with the little girl on his shoulder, he
also took off his hat, his brows branched and
blossomed, and he could not help remembering
that statue of Moses he had seen in a shop window
with the little horns rising from its forehead ;
they were barren, shrivelled to dry bone, they
would never know anything like this. And as he
looked round him, seeing and yet unseeing, it was
transubstantiated bodies that he beheld everywhere ; and it did not matter that on many of
those faces were the marks once traced in some
other world by greed and humiliating servitude
and resentment and degradation, that many of
the women's bodies were shapeless, as though
they had been broken into several pieces and
clumsily put together again : it did not matter,

for all outward semblance was inessential, all
distinction had fallen away like a heavy burden
borne in some other place ; all substance had
been transmuted. And although the pot-bellied
man by his side spoke to him now and then, and
he replied, he could not have told what was said ;
for words too had lost all distinction and become
transparent in this state where speech and silence
had equal meaning.

They passed the crumbling houses of the
Saltmarket, where women in shawls and men in
mufflers stood at the close mouths and stared at
them, and it seemed to Mansie that they too were
changed, in spite of their jeering laughter, and
that only one little thing was needed, a thing
as easy as the lifting of a finger, for all those men
and women to join the procession, to step on to
the floating island and be in bliss ; and he thought
of the hooligans in Eglinton Street : he would
have liked them to be here too ; there was room
for all. Even when the procession reached the
Glasgow Green and that great harmonious being
voluntarily broke its body as for some unknown
sacrament, crumbled for some mysterious and
beneficent purpose into isolated souls again –
even then the spell did not lose its power, and
Mansie wandered from platform to platform,
where Socialist orators, still transfigured so
that he scarcely recognised them, spoke of
the consummated joys of the future society

where all people would live together in love
and joy.

It was only in the evening, when everything
was over and he was walking home, that he
began to wonder whether he had talked a great
deal of nonsense during the day; but even that
fear did not trouble him, for everything was
allowed. He was almost glad that Bob had not
been able to come, and that he had plunged into
this business by himself. As he walked up
Eglinton Street he thought: Nothing can be
the same again. And passing the great red-
haired woman standing at the end of her close,
he did not make his usual detour, skirting the
edge of the pavement, but kept straight on,
almost brushing her with his shoulder. Nor
did the young hooligans bristling on the pavement have any power to harm him now; yet
as he wanted to please even them he stepped
eagerly and with a smile into the street when he
came to them, and though one of them asked
truculently: "What the hell are you girning
at?" all Mansie could do was to go on smiling,
until another of the youths interposed: "Let
the young fella alane. He hasna' hurt you,
has he?"

But when Mansie opened the kitchen door and
saw Tom sitting by the fire in gloomy and rock-
like apathy, it was as though he had run his head
against a wall; he paused irresolutely at the door

and then went through to the parlour and stood looking out at the people passing. As he watched them his blissful security slowly came back. He stood like this for a long time.

I I

Und dass mein eignes Ich, durch nichts gehemmt,
Herüberglitt aus einem kleinen Kind,
Mir wie ein Hund unheimlich stumm und fremd
                    HUGO VON HOFMANNSTHAL

AT FIRST it seemed to Mansie that the revelation
vouchsafed him on May Day must last for ever.
As it happened the first blow to it came in a few
days and from those who had shared it with
him. On Wednesday evening he eagerly set
out for the Clarion Scout rooms. But when he
ran up the stairs and burst into the rooms the
atmosphere of enveloping acceptance was not
there to meet him ; nobody paid any attention
to him ; in the twinkling of an eye they had
all dwindled to their former size again ; they
had all fallen back ; and Sunday and all that had
happened in it might never have been ! He
wandered dejectedly from group to group.
They were discussing the procession : apparently
it had been a disappointment. Mansie listened,
at first with bewilderment, then with interest,
then to his surprise with pleasure, for as his

exaltation of the last few days gradually oozed out of him and he returned to a more comfortable size it was actually a relief – he couldn't but admit it to himself, it was an undeniable relief, though it left a sort of empty feeling somewhere. His feet were on the earth again. Strange how easily you slipped back into your old feelings ! And when a man turned round to him and asked how he had liked his first procession, he said carelessly : " Oh, it was quite all right in its way."

Yet when he left the Clarion Scout rooms he felt cheated and at a loss. The best part of the evening still lay before him, and all at once it seemed quite blank – he had nothing to occupy himself with ; an evening wasted ! So he resolved to walk home. But coming to Eglinton Street and seeing all those people fallen back again, all those dirty children still crying to the heavens – they would cry for a jolly long time before they got any answer, poor little beggars ! – it was more than he could bear ; and at the strident voice of an open air evangelist at the first street corner he abruptly crossed to the other side and waited for a tramcar to take him home. As he sat on the top of the tram he reviewed again his feelings on May Day, and now they filled him with alarm. Something far wrong with the whole business ; something soft and sticky, almost indecent ! The disciple laying his head on the other's breast rose into his mind; he had been jolly near doing that himself, by gum! Almost made a complete ass of himself. What would the people he knew have said if they had seen him? And a still earlier memory stirred insinuatingly in the grounds of his mind. But he pitilessly repressed it : an unhealthy-minded, unnatural young beggar he must have been then! Had to take care. Dangerous to let yourself go like that. That fat man he had walked beside in the procession, couldn't even remember now what he had said to him, might have said anything, given himself away hopelessly. The disturbing memory stirred again, rose a little, vague and sickly, and seemed to float down his mind like the procession floating down Glassford Street, becoming involved with the rising and falling shoulders, which now gave him a sensation almost of sea-sickness. He would take dashed good care that he didn't go to another May Day ! But all the time he was on the tramcar he could not get that early memory out of his mind.

It was a quite vague memory, and concerned an affair that he had had, and should not have had, with a little girl from a neighbouring farm when he was six. He had had no consciousness of guilt, or only a sense of it as purely fanciful as the comedy he was playing ; and indeed, seeing that sex was still unawakened in him, and he was only acting, he was probably as innocent of any actual or even possible offence as a character playing an enigmatic part in a story. Yet he had felt environed by guilt, and this had made him carry out his games in secrecy. At certain stages children seem to live in two separate worlds, both of which are real. In one world, the world which included his parents and all other grown people and himself, a place perfectly familiar to them but full of perplexities for him, Mansie knew that what he did was, in spite of its simplicity, a sin of awful dimensions; but in the other country where he lived with his playmate there was no evil, or a purely fictitious evil which he could summon before his mind only by make-believe. So accompanying the clear knowledge that he was disobeying his father and mother, was the feeling that he was committing a fabulous sin, a sin which was not a sin to him, but to some shadowy figure – it might be God – in a world only visible to his elders.

In his memory, and more especially during the years of adolescence, this episode seemed to him, grotesquely enough, the most shameful in all his life. He could no longer remember the feelings that had accompanied his acts, and he seemed to himself simply to have been a very nasty and unnatural little boy. Unnatural, for now he could only see those games, played in a world where the powers of sex were still unawakened, and so non-existent, through the eyes of a youth whose thoughts were penetrated with sex and his awareness of it, and in this distorting medium his childish play acquired not only a shadow of perversity, but even something of the disgrace of impotence ; and when, after joining the Clarion Scouts, someone told of the agapemones of the early Christians, those promiscuous love-feasts in which lust seemed so strangely mingled with piety, innocence with vice, universal love with sexual perversity, that period of his childhood wavered up before him again. The forms taken by his games, however, were by then almost completely effaced from his mind, and all that remained was a thickly-woven cloud, corporeally oppressive, and both bright and dense, like a golden nightmare weighing on his mind. Yet at the same time he felt that this cloud lay deeper in childhood than any other memory he could summon, lay there, ring-shaped, in an almost terrifyingly secure and still zone, at that very heart of childhood into which it is perilous even for children to venture too far. Its radiance was richer than the light on the little green hill behind the house where he had lain so often and watched the ships passing over the sound in the shadow of the black islands – passing so slowly that he could discern no motion in them, and yet saw, with a feeling of wonder, that they had moved. The

towering hills changing from black to dark blue
of the neighbouring isle, the little red coat with
the yellow buttons – a red and yellow so absolute
that they seemed to exist not as mere qualities but
as living things, quivering like flames and glowing
like flowers : these he remembered vividly ; yet
they faded almost to the hue of an ordinary
memory if the thought came to him of that rich
and bright cloud in which, as in a trance, some
part of him for ever beyond his reach still
lay imprisoned ; so that the memory awoke in
him a vague need to struggle and free himself from something or other, he did not know
what.

He and his playmate had already turned to
other games when his father took a farm on the
mainland. And then, without warning, the guilt,
which had been hanging, a small and distant cloud
in the sky, and should with the discontinuance of
the offence have dissolved and vanished, fell
upon him in a clap. It was after the time of the
sheep-dipping. His father had warned them all
against touching the sack in which the sheep-dip
was kept. The sack was laid out in a field at some
distance from the house ; the sheep were dipped,
and the empty sack was burned ; but for a long
time afterwards Mansie could not rid himself of
the obsession that the poison had got on to his
hands. He washed them in terror many times a
day until they had a wasted and transparent look.

At first it was the poison that he tried to cleanse from them; but as time went on he washed them in a panic, as though he were purifying them of something that he had long since forgotten, some mysterious stain which could be erased only for a moment and immediately returned again; like the *Book of Black Arts* which you could drown in the sea or burn in the fire, but would always be found lying in its place in your trunk if you had once been so unfortunate as to possess it. Every day was filled with alarms and trepidations which invisibly lay in ambush and did not leave him even when he slipped suddenly round a corner to avoid them, or locked himself in the dark cupboard where he hoped they could not enter. He did not know from what source they came or what brought them on him; for by now he had completely forgotten the little girl, and when he thought of that time a comforting blank, which yet disturbed him as if it concealed some treachery, was all that his memory gave back. He could not tell his father and mother of his fears, and so they enclosed him in a silent world whose invisible terrors he had to face by himself. The knowledge that there were things in which his parents' help, no matter how anxious, could be of no use to him, bewildered him most of all; the feeling that he lived in a blind place was perpetually with him; yet this blind place was only a thin film surrounding

him, from which if he ran very fast and very
far he might be able to escape; and his cousin
playing a few feet away in the sun, and his mother
taking his own head on her shoulder in the fire-
light, were in that secure world, and yet he was
outside. The only way he could think of escaping
his terrors was by running very fast until he could
run no farther; and when he fell and bruised
himself he felt that the blood trickling down
must, as by an expiatory rite, bring him back to
the ordinary world where other children too
bruised their knees and bled. But these accidents
staved off his invisible alarms only for a little, and
deceived him.

This period in his life was one of real and
urgent terror. How long it lasted he could not
tell now, but it must have been towards the end,
when his fears were thinning, and twisted gleams
of the real world appeared again as through
running glass, that his mother had taken him
out to the back of the house to see the lamb. He
had been ill, of what he could not remember,
and this was his first day out. As between two
folds of cloud he could still see the black lamb
beside its mother against the spring sky. The
lamb was weak and tottered as it ran; the soft
black wool covering its gawky body, the lac-
quered little cloven hoofs, the soft eyes, which
still had a bruised look, appeared to have been
just made; and the lamb seemed both surprised

and glad to be on the earth. And suddenly, as though it had come for this, a black lamb cast up without warning on the green sward, it charmed him out of his nightmare, and he saw the young sky and the great world outspread. The lamb paid no attention to him and yet seemed aware of him ; it played like a child who feels its mother's eyes upon it and in its inward dream is telling her something which it wants her to know. The dark cloud returned again, but soon after this it must have vanished.

So Mansie sat on the top of the tramcar smoking a cigarette ; and the ship passed and did not pass, the little red coat glowed and glittered, the two hands cleansed each other and yet were not cleansed. And over all hung the ring of golden cloud with two long lost figures, himself and the little girl, hidden at its heart, hidden there and past all help. He shrugged his shoulders as if shaking himself free of something, he did not know what. But even while he did so he felt his helplessness. Somewhere beyond his control the ring-shaped cloud of childhood touched the ring that had encircled him as he floated in bliss on his island down the stony defiles of the streets of Glasgow, touched it and melted into it ; and now he could scarcely tell what filled him with such apprehension, the apprehension evoked by things born irrevocably before their time, or made of too soft and perishable substance. He resolved again, definitely, never to go to another May Day.

12

DURING the winter Mansie and Helen had been assiduously attending Socialist dances and whist drives. Helen had hesitated at first, but when she was at last persuaded to go to one of the monthly dances given by the Clarion Scouts, the number of well-dressed people, the liberal sprinkling of evening suits and smart low-necked ball dresses, reassured, impressed, even a little awed her; and besides during the evening Mansie introduced her to several school-teachers of both sexes. She was agreeably surprised; it was clear that a girl who respected herself could come here without fearing that she might regret it; indeed she felt that she had risen several steps in the social scale, and so – for that is invariably the corollary of such a feeling – was delighted to have at last found her true level. If doubts recurred during the evening, when she came in contact, during a set of quadrilles or lancers, with the more proletarian elements, she was immediately reassured, say, by some white-haired old lady, obviously of superior station, who sat regarding with good-humoured amusement the

rude but well-meant antics of the more obvious
working class ; and these rough men and stern-
looking women, of whom she would have been
slightly afraid otherwise, became harmlessly
transformed into a chorus of comic yokels in a
play ; there was no real harm in them, they were
doing their best, and before the evening ended
she too was smiling experimentally at them,
conscious that that was the right thing to do in
this more elegant and emancipated society into
which she had stepped.

It was a revelation ; and there was nothing
now to prevent Mansie and Helen from flinging
themselves into a whirl of dances and whist
drives that lasted the whole winter. And as
though that exhilarating rush of movement were
a revolving fan winnowing the chaff from the
grain, its last revolution cast them strangely
clean and light into the lap of an early spring. It
may have been merely the discovery that things
which they had hitherto regarded as wicked
were not only permitted, not only harmless, but
good for one ; in any case the whole atmosphere
of their thoughts and feelings cleared, the
brooding twilight which had meant happiness to
them at one time rolled back, some life process
reversed its course, and they found themselves
in calm and luminous light, the light of a sunny
Saturday afternoon. They were happy without
misgiving : that was all. The faint shadow of

apprehension that had darkened all their pleasures, that had made even dancing an enjoyment
to be indulged sparingly if one were not to tempt
providence, had been danced clean away. They
had danced themselves into a new world.

But though it was dancing that most radically
transformed their ideas, some credit must also be
given to Socialist thought. Yet even that they
seemed to absorb more through their bodies than
their minds; and while they whirled on the
smooth floors of a consecutive flight of bril-
liantly-lit ballrooms, from the throng of other
couples revolving round them were flung out
radiating intellectual sparks which softly pelted
them and in course of time adhered; so that
without knowing how it had come about they
presently found themselves convinced that the
world belonged to mankind, and that in collabora-
tion with mankind they might seek and con-
fidently expect to find happiness there. They
seemed to possess far more things than they had
ever done before, but they were quite unable to
distinguish between those that were actual and
those that were merely potential; for if anything
the latter were the more real to them, and gave
them a pleasure quite as solid as corporeal
substances could have done. For suddenly all
the suffering in the world, all the evils which
they had once accepted as ordained, were revealed
as remediable – things that could be " abolished ";

and for their liberated minds, still a little dizzy at
the new prospect, the step from the possibility
of a remedy to the accomplished cure was a short
and dreamlike one, and they might be easily
forgiven for taking it. With half their minds,
the half that was freed when their day's work
was done, they lived in the future as some
people, especially in youth, live in poetry or in
music; and so, breathing in anticipation the
more spacious air of the coming Socialist state,
they had no need to con books on economics,
thick volumes which in any case the consummation of Socialism itself would providentially
abolish; no more need than they had to open the
works of Nietzsche and Shaw to acquaint themselves with the attributes of the Superman, seeing
that they already felt far closer affinities with him,
as merely another inhabitant of the future, a
sort of neighbour, than with the provisionary
phenomenon of mankind. And if it had not
been that all young Socialists of his time without
exception read Edward Carpenter's *Love's Coming
of Age*, Mansie would not have read that either;
for any limitation of his floating ideas, even on
free love, was an interruption of his undifferenti-
ated delight, a violation, a disfigurement. And
in fact Mansie was shocked by the book, and
did not hand it to Helen after all when he was
finished with it. He was still more shocked than
he had been one evening when a clever young

fellow in the Clarion Scouts told him that,
according to Nietzsche, the Superman would be
as different from man as man was from the
monkeys. The idea displeased Mansie; that
wasn't how he saw it in his own mind at all. He
felt he disagreed with Nietzsche.

Yet all this dwelling in the future did not lessen
Mansie's benevolent friendship for mankind, or
for the trifling part of it that he met; and if the
future revealed a world in which humanity, every
evil abolished, was at last free and glorified, it
was in unjust social conditions that the decency
of decent fellows shone most eminently, and he
still felt that he was surrounded by a great host
of decent fellows. Indeed now they seemed more
decent than ever, for his vision of a transfigured
humanity cast a reflected radiance back upon their
faces, and sometimes he could see in a flash how
gloriously they would shine out if poverty and
adversity and dulling toil and servitude were
lifted from them. It was like a pain at his heart.
Why should such things be? Why should
injustice and hate and suffering and strife con-
tinue? Why should not Socialism come now,
in the twinkling of an eye, and put the world's
sorrows to rest?

In the spring they went for rambles into the
country, sometimes with the Clarion Scouts,
sometimes with a more select party made up for
the occasion. Bob Ryrie often went with them,

and Helen was charmed by his gentlemanly
attentiveness, which made her feel that with his
eyes he was supporting her in the mere act of
walking, helpfully assisting her to climb over
any stile, it did not matter how low, anxiously
hoping that she would enjoy her ramble – as if
he were responsible for it, the absurd fellow!
His brown eyes with their protective glance
enveloped her warmly, and even his brown
tweeds, which gave out the delicatest aroma of
tobacco and peat, were like a soft buffer against
every shock, and she felt secure and irresponsible
behind them. To Mansie Bob was enthusiastic
about her. " A superior girl ! " he said, and it
was at his suggestion that Mansie ceased to take
her to the Clarion Scout rambles. " A bit rough
and tumble," Bob said. " Playing football in a
field's all right for you and I, even if it's on a
Sunday. But for a refined girl like Helen——"
So they made up a small party every Sunday and
went out to Strathblane or the Mearns. They
were very happy.

Yet though such a revolutionary change had
taken place within Mansie and Helen, anyone
perusing their actions would not have found any
sign of it, for conduct too lay for them in the
future. So although they devoutly believed in
free love it never entered their minds to put it
into practice ; and had Mansie attempted any of
the liberties with Helen which had caused Tom's

downfall, she would have been just as indignant again, in spite of her emancipated ideas ; still more indignant, indeed, for she had fled to Mansie as a refuge from those very perils. But she had no need to fear Mansie. For in this atmosphere disinfected by the future, an atmosphere generated by Ibsen, Shaw, Nietzsche, Carpenter and Wells, but whose fantastic possibility was unbounded even by that fact, for Mansie had not even read those writers, it became quite easy to dissipate in an ever wider concentric circle every impulse that was urgent or painful, to vaporise oneself until one was conscious of no residue. Never before had Maisie felt so free.

When a disturbing fact, a case of objective suffering, an illness, say, in the family, impinges on the consciousness of anyone in Mansie's state, at first it is a distant and muffled sound heard by the physical ear while the mind is securely asleep, and for a while the mind tries to weave it into its dream. Until the moment comes when the phantom shadow becomes so gigantic and affrighting, so far more oppressive than the objective fact itself, that with a start the sleeper awakes.

13

ONE EVENING a few weeks after the May Day procession Mansie was sitting at the kitchen window reading the evening paper until it should be time to go out. Tom was crouching over the fire with his elbows on his knees and his head in his hands. His presence did not disturb Mansie, for though they still did not speak to each other all the tension had gone out of their silence; and even when, as sometimes happened, they brushed shoulders as they passed each other in the lobby, that was a mere chance which could not be avoided in a small flat.

Tom gave a muffled groan now and then, but even that did not disturb Mansie very greatly; it must be one of Tom's headaches, for Tom had been having a great many headaches lately. But when Tom began to rock his head from side to side, still holding it tightly clenched in his hands, and emitting a long quivering sigh that ended in a loud groan, Mansie became alarmed; he laid down the paper on the table and half raised himself from his chair. Should he speak to the fellow? This looked serious! Why had his

mother and Jean gone out this evening of all
evenings ? Perhaps he should really speak to
him ? For Tom's rocking had grown faster now,
it went on and on as if he couldn't stop, as if he
actually didn't know what he was doing. And
Mansie was on the very point of opening his
mouth – this   couldn't   go   on ! – when   Tom
turned an unrecognisable face to him, a blood-
shot face over which some dreadful change
had come, so that it looked like somebody
else's, and gasped : " Get a doctor, for God's
sake ! "

" I'll get one at once ! " Mansie burst out,
almost taking the words out of Tom's mouth. He
should have spoken before ! " I'll get one at
once. . . . What's the matter ? . . . Wouldn't
you feel better lying down ? "

" No, no ! " groaned Tom, and as if speech
had released something he beat his head against
the wall and burst out : " I don't know what it
can be ! I don't know what it can be ! " He
turned a blind face to Mansie, and Mansie saw
with terror that in his wide open eyes the eyeballs
were rolling round and round like wheels that
had flown off their axles.

" Don't do that, Tom ! " he cried. Good God,
what could it be ? " Let me help you across to
the bed." He put his arms under Tom's armpits,
pulled him up, stumbled with him over to the
bed and carefully lowered him, laying his head

on the pillow. He looked back before he rushed out; Tom was lying still.

At the second attempt he found a young doctor who was willing to accompany him. When they entered the kitchen Mrs. Manson and Jean were standing by the bed still wearing their hats and coats.

"What has happened, Mansie?" said Mrs. Manson. Her face was white and she looked at him reproachfully. The doctor went forward to the bed. Mansie told what had happened, and involuntarily added: "I don't know what it can be." It sounded almost like an exculpation, but for what?

While she was listening Mrs. Manson kept her eyes fixed on the doctor. The doctor was bent over Tom as if engaged on some secret and sinister task, bent so low that they could not see what he was doing, could see nothing but Tom's crumpled blue trousers and grey stockinged feet.

At last the doctor straightened himself and turned round.

"I think I can give him a powder that will ease the pain," he said, and he turned to Mansie: "You'd better come back with me for it."

"What is it, doctor?" asked Mrs. Manson.

"To be honest, Mrs. Manson, I can't say yet. I'll have to give him a second examination to-morrow. No need for worry meantime. The powder will put him to sleep." And the doctor made resolutely for the door.

Outside he turned to Mansie. "I'll tell you what I would like," he began in quite a different tone. "I would like your brother to go into the Western Infirmary for observation for a week or two."

Mansie's heart sank. The infirmary! Could it be as bad as that?

"Will you try to persuade your mother that it's the best thing to do? He'll be well looked after and quite comfortable."

Mansie promised with a sinking heart. After a pause the doctor asked: "What sort of life has your brother led?"

A queer question to ask a fellow! Mansie replied: "He's an engineer by trade."

"That wasn't what I meant. I've a definite reason for asking, and you can help me by being perfectly frank. Did he go about with women a lot?"

Mansie's face grew red. He looked at the people passing as though he were afraid they had heard.

"No. He had a girl once, but they haven't been keeping company for some time now." Why had he said that? A stupid thing to say!

But the doctor still persisted. What *was* he getting at? "Can you tell me whether he ever

went with – er – loose women ? " then as if
taking a plunge, " with prostitutes ? "

" My brother would never do such a thing ! "
Mansie burst out. These doctors ! Bad as the
nurses, the way they spoke about things. But he
felt relieved ; if the doctor connected Tom's
headache with that he was quite off the track.

There was silence again, and then the doctor
asked, as if casually ; " I noticed a slight scar
on his head. How was that caused ? "

As if it had been waiting for this question
Mansie's heart stopped. If it should turn out
to be that fall from the tramcar this might be
serious, by gum ! He told the doctor what
had happened. But the doctor merely said :
" Well, all that I can do at present is to give him
a powder. But make it clear to your mother that
he should go into hospital for observation."

When Mansie returned Tom was already
feeling a little better ; he took the powder
obediently and was soon asleep. Standing by
the bedside Mrs. Manson turned to Mansie and
said gravely : " I'm afraid this is a serious matter,
Mansie." Why did she look at him like that
again ? What had he done ? Still it was good,
in a way, that she should take it seriously ; it
would make the doctor's suggestion less of a
shock. And after standing out for a time she
agreed at last to Tom's going into the Western
Infirmary.

A week later Tom was taken there, and a suspended calm, the calm that follows an inconclusive crisis, descended on the house. Tom was in good and secure hands, Mansie reflected; that was one comfort at any rate. But when one evening, while they were alone in the kitchen, Jean turned to him and said : " Mansie, what if it's a tumour on the brain ? " he burst out angrily, " Don't talk such nonsense ! " It was indecent to say such things. He got up abruptly, stuck on his hat, and left the house.

14

AFTER leaving the office Mansie parted from Gibson, saying: "I'm going along to the Reformers' Bookstall." He would put off the journey for a little while at least. But instead of making for the bookstall he wandered down Hope Street. It was deserted, for all the law offices were already closed. A belated message-boy, a sheaf of blue envelopes in one hand, hurried past him with the anxious look of one who has fallen so far behind in a race that he has lost all his companions. Mansie's own anxiety stirred somewhere, threatened to awaken, then sank again.

He walked on in the chasm of shadow between the tall buildings; but when he came to the corner of West George Street he stepped into a level drive of light; the roofs and smokeless chimney-pots glittered, and looking down the hill he saw a yellow tramcar floating past amid a hurrying crowd of men and girls in bright dresses. And anxiety came over him again. He would have to take that tramcar some time; he couldn't put it off indefinitely! Nevertheless he continued on

his way, went into the Central Station and stood
at the bookstall, his head half-turned to look at
the crowds hurrying to their separate platforms.
They seemed all to be flying to one point, like
filings drawn by an enormous magnet. After
the morning dispersion which had scattered them
to their distant outposts, evening was gathering
them together again, and on the faces that passed
him there was a look : " We are coming." Yes,
it was all very well for them. He thought of
Tom and stood staring at a book on the stall
which he had noticed there months before, and
its persistent futile presence filled him with
discouragement. " You and me," it seemed to
be saying.

He bought an evening paper and walked out
through the side entrance, crossed Union Street,
climbed on to the open top of a yellow tramcar,
and sat down in the back seat. Now that he
felt himself being irrevocably borne home, he
tried to banish from his mind what he would find
there ; for the twenty minutes that were still left
seemed an invisible suit of mail which, if he
refrained altogether from thinking, might soundlessly close round him, encasing him for the
encounter. But it was of no use, for already he
saw himself standing unprepared on the stair-
head with the latch-key in his hand, and the same
feeling that he would have then swept over
him, a sensation of simultaneous collapse, as if

everything within him were loosened and falling, and he himself were being precipitated through the solid stone landing where he stood. He was awakened by a sudden brilliance ; the passengers looked like a glorified company dizzily charging through seas of light : the tramcar was crossing the Jamaica Bridge and the rays of the westering sun showered over it. He looked at the Clyde winding eastwards in radiance, and saw down in the river a fantastically elongated shadow car with a cargo of spectral and aqueous passengers. Beyond the moving shadow ran the little suspension bridge where the noseless beggar had stood. " Eaten away," the words came into Mansie's head. For the wide gaping nose cavity had actually looked as if it were being devoured by incredibly tiny indefatigable armies, and it was against them that the look in the man's face was protesting, and not against the people, all of them with complete faces of every variety of shape, who passed him daily. And his voice ! A subterranean snuffle rising to a soft hoot as of swirling wind in a chimney ; but never any intelligible sound. The poor beggar had stood there in hard frost too. Mansie had always given him a few coppers, though he had had to overcome a physical repulsion first ; and now sitting on the tramcar he remembered that he had been offended at the man for not seeming to be aware of it. Well, a man who had lost his nose couldn't always remember to behave like a man who had lost his nose. Maybe put up his hands sometimes to scratch it, and it wasn't there! A dashed unpleasant shock. But he had looked in a funny accusing way at you sometimes; made you feel uncomfortable. Then he had gone and never appeared again. What could have become of him?

Mansie twisted his shoulders to shake off such disagreeable thoughts. He would fix his mind on something more cheerful; but instead it flew forward to Tom waiting at home, as though the beggar had been cunningly leading him there. Well, there was no good in burking the fact; Tom was out of the hospital now and waiting for him. These fellows sitting here on the top of the tramcar weren't returning to a brother with a tumour on his brain! Idiotic the way Jean's silly words kept running in one's head. He felt all at once violently exasperated with Tom. What need had the silly fool to go and get a tumour on the brain? That was where he landed himself with his dashed recklessness. The tramcar was rolling up through Eglinton Street, and Mansie's eyes fell on the fish-and-chip shop with its door-posts rotten and oozing with rancid grease. He looked to see if the great red-haired woman was standing in the next close as usual, with her arms wrapped round her over-flowing breasts. Yes, she was there, talking to a laughing ring of young girls in shawls, still holding them in; but they would escape some day, and then there would be a fine flop! Nice thoughts to have when your brother was. But all the same she would always be there, nothing could shift her, just like something you had to walk round every morning and evening, forced you out of your way, until at last you got used to your new road and it seemed the natural one. He remembered Gibson's words again: " And what about the poor bloody little children ? " A blackened steel railway-bridge rushed smoothly towards him and passed over his head. The tram-car stopped at Eglinton Toll and turned up Victoria Road. Suddenly like a gaseous fluid dread pumped itself into him, filling him up so tightly that there seemed no room left for the air he tried to draw into his lungs. Four stops, and he would have to get off.

He descended and walked very slowly up Garvin Street. Dashed nonsense! Tom was getting better. At the close mouth he stopped again. Half of him was still out in the street, and to draw it back to him from its freedom, which he shared as a poor man, standing at the lodge gates, shares a fine estate, – to force this half of him to coalesce with the other which was about to walk resolutely into the close and up the stairs, was a task for which he had to summon all his strength as for the pulling in of a heavy weight. With a jerk he turned and climbed the stairs to the first floor. There he was, standing with the key in his hand; but the sensation of sinking through the floor did not come; he had paid that debt in the tramcar; and now his mind was strangely clear, so that when he inserted the key in the lock and turned it his act seemed a purely intellectual one, faintly suggesting the shining revolutions of the stars. As he hung up his hat in the lobby he felt quite indifferent to his brother. "What must be, must," he thought, and walked into the kitchen: "Well, Tom? Feeling better?"

Tom was sitting at the table eating ham and eggs and drinking tea, and at that prosaic sight Mansie's mind fell through octave after octave until it rested on something like reassurance.

"Yes, I think I am," Tom answered with his mouth full.

Mansie took his place at the other side of the table and glanced at his brother. He was astonished. He had expected some change, but this was a clean knock-out. Tom had grown fat. His thin face with the daring line of the cheek-bone and jaw was round and soft now, and the skin seemed darker and coarser, as if there were an admixture of infinitesimal specks of mud in the grain.

Mrs. Manson set a cup of tea and a plate of ham and eggs before Mansie.

" Isna' he changed, Mansie? " she asked. " Isna' he looking weel? "

Tom made a movement with his hand as if he were warding off something.

" But you are looking better, Tom."

" Well, don't make such a song about it, mother," said Tom as if ashamed. " You might talk about something else."

" But I'm that blithe about it ! "

Mansie unobtrusively studied his brother. Something queer about the fellow's face; yes, must be the eyes. Tom's eyes had an intent, almost pleased look, as if he were listening to something inside him : something ticking – Mansie could not keep the thought out of his head – ticking and ticking. Suddenly on this face that he was studying a very quick spasm ran from eye to chin. But it did not seem real somehow ; and indeed it was not caused by real pain, but perhaps by a faintly vibrating memory, even a dream of pain. Yet Mansie felt profoundly cast down all at once ; it had looked almost like a threat. Then the expression of intent and pleased watching returned again. So might a condemned man sitting in chains listen to the rain beating on the window of his cell, and tell himself that so long as he listened to that regular drumming no harm could come to him, for when it was raining – raining as it might rain on any day – how could anything happen, how could the blow fall? And he did not know why, Mansie felt disquieted by that pleased expression on Tom's face.

The evening light was streaming in through the window on to the table. Mansie shifted nervously every now and then to get out of it, and its warmth on the backs of his hands was like a spidery film that he longed to tear away. His mother sat in her chair by the empty range looking into Tom's face. Mansie felt apprehensive, almost scared, at the expression in her eyes, for although of course Tom would get better it was almost asking for trouble to be as confident as that. His heart sank at the thought that the pain might return after all, and pushing back his chair he walked to the window. There, looking out into the backyard as if that put a barrier between him and his brother, he said : " So the pain's quite gone now ? "

His mother threw him a warning look, but Tom replied quite coolly : " Yes, I haven't had any for more than a fortnight now." Mansie asked him how he had liked the nurses ; a queer lot, from all accounts.

" Oh, they're all right," said Tom indifferently.

" Well, you'll just let your mother look after you now, my lamb," said Mrs. Manson. " We'll have the whole hoose to oursel's. You'll get up when you like, and we'll live like grand folk."

" All right, mother," said Tom impatiently.

Then as if he had something really important to discuss he turned to Mansie : " They told me I was to go for walks. Have you anything on this evening ? "

" No, nothing. I'll take you—— I'll go for a stroll with you if you like."

In the lobby Tom turned to Mansie with a pleased look : " I've been putting on weight. Twelve pounds ! "

As they were walking along Garvin Street Mansie thought he noticed something queer about Tom's walk, but told himself that he must be mistaken. At the corner of Victoria Road Tom stopped and carefully surveyed the street before crossing. They wandered slowly in the direction of the Queen's Park recreation grounds. And now Mansie saw – and his heart almost stopped – that Tom was really walking very strangely. His feet, flung out with the old impetuousness, seemed to hang in the air for the fraction of a second before they returned, a little uncertainly, to the ground. It was as though the additional weight of his body had made him a little top-heavy. He walked very carefully with his eyes fixed on the pavement a few steps in front of him, as if there, no nearer and no farther, lay the danger that he must circumvent, a danger that continuously advanced with him as he went on.

From the gate the recreation park stretched before them, in the distance rising to a grassy

sunlit hill, behind which rose the irregular ridged
roofs and chimneys of Mount Florida. In the
eastern sky beyond floated a few pink fleece-like
clouds, deepening at their centres to hectic rose.
Shouts came towards them on the still air, mingled
with the thud of footballs and the sharp click of
bats. They walked over to a seat where they
could watch a game of cricket. And soon the
vigilant inward look had quite faded from Tom's
face ; for now he followed almost with anxiety
the ball as it flew from the bats of the players,
followed it with tortured hope as if in its flight
it might carry him into another world, a world
where everybody's head was as sound as a nut.
This could take him out of himself, Mansie was
thinking, and his mother couldn't! " Tits,
man. Hit it! Hit it! " Tom kept muttering
impatiently. A band of schoolboys were running
about, and sometimes in swerving they almost
knocked against the seat. For long intervals
they would play at the other side of the field ;
then for a little they would circle round the seat
as persistently as a swarm of bees. At last Tom
muttered in a tearful voice : " Go away, damn
you ! Go away ! " The boys were back again.
Suddenly, just in front of Mansie, one of them
tottered and fell and Mansie saw a cricket ball
bounding away at a tangent. The boys stood
round, quite silent all at once, the batsman came
running across. Tom got hastily to his feet and

said : " Come away ! It isn't safe here." Mansie rose and followed him.

" Fine rotters you are ! " the batsman panted, bending over the boy. " Walking away when you see someone hurt ! "

" My brother's ill," said Mansie.

" Oh ! Sorry ! "

Mansie turned back to see if he could help. The boy was lying on the grass, his face transparent, his breath [quick and soft as if he were inhaling an infinitely subtle atmosphere. He looked like someone to whom something fortunate but very strange had happened.

The batsman raised his head : " Run to the pump for some water ! Here's my cap. Hurry!"

One of the boys flew away.

" It hit him here," said another, pointing to his collar-bone.

The batsman felt the neck of the unconscious boy with his fingers. " No bones broken. It must have been the shock." And as though those words were a magical formula, his voice was quite confident now. He wiped the sweat from his face. The boy opened his eyes, which had a bruised and wandering look.

" All right again ? " asked the batsman in a matter-of-fact voice.

" I suppose I can go now," said Mansie. Without waiting for an answer he walked across to Tom.

" Where did it hit him ? "

" On the collar-bone. He'll be all right in a little. He fainted."

" It's lucky for him it didn't catch him on the head ! Serve him right. These damned kids shouldn't be out playing so late as this, anyway."

Tom walked on. The accident was merely an accident, and soon the boy would be walking about again, none the worse. At the thought he felt the disease within his head like a grub clinging to him. He would never be able to shake it off, and yet he did not know what it was or where it was ; he put up his hand to the back of his skull, which was hard and blank, like a wall. " And it might have hit me on the head ! " He did not notice that he had spoken the words aloud until Mansie gave him a warning glance. He walked on faster, his left leg swinging out jerkily. All at once his head seemed terribly vulnerable ; a slate might fall on it from a house-roof, a chance stone flung by a boy might hit it. Or he might stumble and fall and ruin everything now that he was getting better. The sweat broke out on him. I've got to be very careful, he thought, at this stage. He jerked Mansie back by the sleeve. " Can't you wait a bit·! Don't you see there's a car coming ? " They were at the corner of Victoria Road. A tramcar was slowly approaching from the direction of the park gates; it was still a good distance away. Presently it ground past them, continuously pulverising some invisible and piteous object which hovered just above the dust in front of it, and Tom felt the pavement thrilling with a menace that had been and was over. They crossed the empty street.

"You've got to be careful when you've just come out of hospital," Tom said half-apologetically. "A pretty poor game, wasn't it?" But immediately his thoughts closed him in again, and Mansie's reply was cast back as from a wall.

"Come in and sit down!" Mrs. Manson cried as soon as they entered the kitchen.

"I'm going to bed, mother," said Tom coldly. "The doctor told me to get as much sleep as possible."

"Ay, just do that, lamb."

Mansie went through to the parlour and stood looking out of the window. He breathed quickly as though he had been running, and an intense longing drew him to everything his eyes fell on: an old man walking peacefully along the pavement, the windows opposite with their dingy lace curtains, the impalpable white sky. He felt hollow and cold, as if all the warmth in his body were being drained out through the glass panes into the street below him, and was wandering homelessly there like a lost dog eager to attach itself to any master. Eglinton Street. The pavement was coated with a thick layer of liquid mud, into which one's feet sank with a humiliating feeling of discomfort and shame. A frightening place, Glasgow! Every winter his father's farm had been like a thin raft riding on nothing but clay and mud. Terrible clinging mud; but he had escaped, he had found a firm foothold on the dry clean streets of Blackness. If he were only back there again! He felt tired out as though he had been walking and walking to get to the end of Eglinton Street, to get past all those houses, all those people who kept looking at you.

He began to walk up and down the room. Must get out of this! His mother came in.

"He's going to bed," she whispered. "Did he say anything to you?"

"No. He didn't say much."

"Isna' he looking better?"

"Yes.—Mother, I think I'll go out for a turn."

"Why? Have you an engagement? Come in quietly, then, and be sure not to waken him."

She was offended. He turned to the window: the light was running away from him as through a sand-glass. His mother's soft footsteps receded. He stole into the lobby and softly closed the outside door behind him.

He hastened up Victoria Road. The park was still open: thank God, the park was still open! For a moment he had half thought of going to the Clarion Scout rooms, for he wanted to lose himself among people and wash away the remoteness with which Tom had touched him. But the park with its trees, its flowers and its crowds, all sending out the same glow, drew him unresistingly. Inside the gate he was caught by the crowd coming away from the band enclosure; he let himself be carried along by the weight of the massed bodies round him, his limbs became slack as under a stream of warmth, and life ran back into his veins. He went up the main avenue and turned along the terraced gardens, from which the scents were pouring in a steady stream, perfuming all the air, perfuming his very breath. Once more his arms and head seemed to break into blossom, and it was as though he were floating, an anonymous shape, in the half-darkness. From the blacker shadows came low voices and now and then a laugh which seemed startled at its own sound; and a warmth radiated out to him from the populated darkness, and he was glad that he could wander here alone, without Helen. And again the warmth of his body flowed out, but freely and blissfully now, filling the twilight, stretching from horizon to horizon, a web as perfect and delicate as the tissue of a moth's wing, except for one point, a point no bigger than a burn made by a red-hot needle, a blackened point of which as he walked on he was scarcely aware, so distant and so tiny did it seem. But when he emerged from the

tree-shaded gardens to barer ground and saw the
street lamps far away in Pollokshaws Road, that
distant harsh burning leapt so viciously at him
that he turned round hastily into the scented
darkness again.   But now the park-keepers'
whistles blew ; a rustling came from the trees ;
voices that a moment before had sounded sweet
or care free all at once became matter-of-fact, and
the laughter had a note of embarrassment.   It
was over.   They were going home, just going
home, after all.   Surely the park-keepers might
have waited for a little longer ?   Mansie mingled
with the crowd moving towards the gate.   It
seemed to be carrying him irresistibly on a wave
from which there was no escape, and which must
inevitably wash him up on that stair-head, where
he could do nothing – nothing at all – but take
the key out of his pocket and turn it in the lock.
A fine life for a fellow !   How long was this to
last ?

15

To be seen out walking in the company of a man with a physical infirmity makes one self-conscious, it may be even a little ashamed, as one is ashamed of an acquaintance who is shabbily dressed. But if the man should be your brother the matter touches you far more nearly, and you may actually have the feeling that there is something wrong with your own clothes. You take off your bowler hat with a puzzled and absent air and run your palm round it to make sure that the polish has not been tarnished; your stiff collar feels uncomfortable; and when anyone passes you stare carelessly ahead as if nothing were the matter and perhaps throw a casual remark to your companion, signifying by your unconcern that nothing is really the matter with him either, whatever appearances may say.

If your companion's infirmity is one that makes it obviously unsafe for him to be out alone, your self-consciousness may become acute. You fancy that people are staring suspiciously at you. "Something wrong here," their eyes seem to be saying; "that poor fellow should be at home or in hospital." And when they see what pains he is taking to walk smartly, as though nothing were the matter, planting his heels on the ground with jerky regularity, and reminding one of nothing so much as a sergeant-major blind to the world dazedly upholding the dignity of the British Army, they look reproachfully at you as though you were wantonly making a public exhibition of this friend of yours, whoever he is.

But this is only at the beginning of your apprenticeship, and soon you discover that there are other people who glance at you with interest and sympathy, first at your companion and then at you, clearly thinking : "A good, kind-hearted young fellow, that." They are mostly men whose hair is turning grey ; but women of all ages also notice you, and the eyes of the younger ones seem to be saying : "What a pity that that poor young fellow's life should be wasted in looking after a helpless invalid!" And if the girl is pretty, sometimes you sadly return her look, return it without the slightest danger that she will think you are trying to pick her up ; for the society you are keeping now makes you immune, puts you indeed in what might almost be called a privileged position. So you can woo as many pretty eyes as you like without any risk of encountering either disdain or, what would be almost shocking, coy encouragement. Still, being a decent fellow, you sometimes feel a little

ashamed of being the sole target of this battery
of sweet glances, and would like to deflect some
of them to your companion, who needs them far
more than you do. Then you cannot help half-
turning towards him, feel tempted indeed to
raise your hand and wave it in his direction, like
a performer in the theatre wafting half the
applause to his assistant, without whom he could
do nothing. But your assistant never receives
a single glance. Women are really a queer lot !

Yet this, you know all the time, is only on the
surface ; all this is unreal : the running fire of
sweet glances no less than your rôle to which
they are merely the response ; the reproving stares
of respectable citizens no less than the hang-dog
air with which they immediately saddle you ;
for all the time it is your brother Tom who is
spasmodically strutting there by your side, and
all the time you are Mansie Manson. None of
those people know that, none of them can ever
know what that means ; for it is a truth so simple
and irreducible that if you were to try to explain
it you could only repeat your original words
again ; a secret so securely sealed that even if you
gathered all the people in the Queen's Park
together and proclaimed it publicly to them, they
would be no wiser.

And so as Mansie Manson walked by his
brother's side in the warm summer evenings
through the Queen's Park or the recreation

grounds, he could freely think of whatever came into his mind, respond to glances, put on an interesting or an unconcerned air; for that was all secondary and idle, so deeply was he aware the whole time that this was his brother Tom and that he himself was Mansie Manson. Even his shame at feeling ashamed of walking here in public with his brother was idle; it was a detached and objective response which did not really touch him; he felt it almost by an act of choice; and it seemed to him that if he cared to make a different choice he would not feel it at all. And the fact that he could quite calmly think of Helen too, and plan where he would take her next evening, was equally idle, seeing that in any case he had to occupy his mind with something. For Tom left him completely to himself, left him far more alone than he would have been unaccompanied; by his absorption in himself Tom seemed to be silently imploring him for heaven's sake to discover something of his own to think about, it did not matter what. For all that Tom wanted was to escape notice, to ignore and be ignored, so that in peace he might listen to that internal ticking which reassured him so profoundly, and keep his eyes steadily fixed on the path a few steps in front of him, where lay, no nearer and no farther, the risk that he must avoid.

Yet there were bounds to this suspended

freedom in which Mansie walked beside his
brother, and they were reached when in musing
over Helen he remembered with quickened pulses
the savour of her kisses and the contact of her
body. It was as though a peril had sprung up
at his side, and he would glance quickly at Tom,
terrified for a moment lest Tom had guessed his
thoughts. And, his eyes still hypnotically fixed
on Tom, on the left leg jerking out, hanging in
the air for the fraction of a second and returning
a little uncertainly to the ground, he would think,
" There's no turning back after this. We must
get married when Tom is well again." It seemed
in a sense their duty to Tom, an acknowledgment
of the greatness of his misfortune. Yes, if they
were to treat this business idly it would be a
wanton insult to Tom. They were bound
together now, and as soon as Tom was well
again they would announce their engagement and
get married. Of course while Tom was ill they
could not even announce their engagement :
Helen agreed with him there. But what if Tom
were never to get quite well ? What if his leg
were to jerk like this for the rest of his life, or
even for the next five years ? They couldn't
postpone their marriage for ever ! After all, it
wasn't as if Tom's illness was their fault. The
position was unfortunate, certainly ; it was a
problem. Well, there was no use in worrying
about it at the moment. Tom would be all right

again, no doubt, in a few months. Ridiculous
notions that came into one's head!

Yet the idea of marriage disturbed Mansie,
and particularly since he had begun to suspect
that Jean and Brand were thinking of it too. For
being married to Jean would be no joke; she
would take it in deadly earnest and she would
make Brand take it in deadly earnest too; she
would stick to him through thick and thin;
" till death do us part "; it absolutely scared
you. No, when you thought of Jean marrying,
you saw that marriage wasn't a bed of roses by
any means; it was a very serious business, almost
terrifying, like joining the army. And yet it
attracted you in a queer way too: burning your
boats. Well, if Helen and he did that, surely
that would wipe off everything. Tom could have
nothing to complain of, surely, after that.

Mansie had only one really uncomfortable
moment during those promenades. As they
were walking through the recreation park one
evening, whom should they meet but Helen.
When she saw them she started visibly and seemed
to be looking round her for something to hide
behind, and in her confusion she actually remained standing where she was. Mansie stopped
too, equally at a loss, and mechanically raised his
hat. A fine figure he cut, standing there with his
hat in his hand! Yet what could a fellow do in
the circumstances, but simply lift his hat? Then

Helen abruptly walked on, and putting his hat
back on his head again Mansie followed Tom,
whose left leg he saw jerking busily in front of
him. Mansie fell in by his side without speaking :
an unfortunate business. Tom's face was red,
and all at once he exclaimed furiously as though
nobody else were there : " The common bitch ! "
And he brought down the point of his stick with
a grinding crunch on the gravel of the path. The
blood rose quite slowly into Mansie's cheeks ;
he felt as he had done at school when he was
reprimanded before the class, felt like a schoolboy who must patiently let his face grow redder
and redder and look more and more foolish
without being able to answer a single word. Yet
he did not resent what Tom had said ; on the
contrary he felt on Tom's side ; there was a
secret between them now from which Helen was
shut out and with which she had no concern ;
and in any case what right had she to fling a
fellow's hair into the sea like that ! He would
never be able to tell her how Tom felt, of course.
Would have to put her off with some story or
other.

Tom made no further comment on the incident,
and their evening walks continued undisturbed.
Bob Ryrie sometimes joined them, and then
Mansie walked along with a still greater feeling
of detachment ; it was as though Tom were
completely taken off his hands, and anyone

passing might have thought that Bob was the solicitous brother and Mansie merely a friend goodnaturedly keeping him company. Of course Brand never volunteered his society; to bother about illness was beneath him, didn't come within his scheme of things, hadn't anything to do with Socialism; yes, to him Tom was just a chap that would never be of any use for the movement. Bob was far more of a Socialist at heart, though he couldn't argue your head off like Brand. A queer fish to think of getting married to. It would be a dashed funny marriage. But if Bob couldn't spout all sorts of theories, he could make Tom talk, and that took some doing. Tom liked his company, cheered up like anything when Bob appeared. Jean, of course, pretended not to notice, never even thanked the fellow; but Bob was never given the credit that he deserved. And walking along Mansie listened to Bob drawing Tom out, telling funny stories, or discussing last season's football form; and for a little they were all happy.

16

THE FIRST few weeks after Tom's return from
hospital passed in a Sabbath calm. All the life in
the house seemed to slow down with the slowing
down of Tom's bodily movements, bringing a
compulsory relaxation in which even anxiety for
the future was lulled to sleep, a sleep which had
to be watched over with bated breath, as one
watches through the protracted crisis of an illness. It was a tension which consisted in a
deliberate avoidance and postponement of tension, and it demanded somewhat the same effort
that is prescribed in exercises for completely re-
laxing the muscles of the body.

Yet although in this Sabbath-like daily com-
munion with her son, serene as the dawn of a new
dispensation, Mrs. Manson drank comfort as
from a fount that had been sealed for many years,
and although the thought that he might never
get better did not enter her mind, often she gazed
at him with sudden alarm. True, Tom's slowness had something restful, something deliberate
and leisurely, as though he were quietly reflecting
on what he should do next – as he had been

doing, for instance, before he got up a minute ago from his chair and walked over to the window to look down into the backyard and up at the sky, where the white June clouds were floating. And it was pleasant to see with what contentment he enjoyed his ease in bed every morning, like a good boy who has been told that he must lie still; and when he got up the leisurely care with which he put on his clothes was pleasant too, he so obviously enjoyed it. It gave one quite a sense of ease and order to see him spending such a long time on everything; on shaving, for instance, and knotting his tie, and brushing his hair. Yet even when that was done, and he had put on his waistcoat and jacket, even then he was not finished. For then he would sit down to a new occupation he had found, one that he kept to the last and seemed to enjoy most of all. Seated erect in his chair by the fireside he would take a little file from his waistcoat pocket and carefully file and polish the nails of his hands, which, after their long idleness, were nearly as white and smooth as Mansie's. And it was when he was busied in occupations as harmless and reassuring as this that Mrs. Manson would gaze across at him in sudden alarm.

The days of a sick man who is able to walk about, dress carefully and attend to his appearance, have something of an aristocratic seclusion

and spaciousness. His infirmity may confine him
to a pair of small rooms, but for the spatial freedom that he is denied, Time, Time in which he
can do nothing at all if he chooses, richly recom-
penses him, translating itself into a new and
more satisfying, because more amenable, dimension of space. And so when, instead of madly
rushing through the far-stretching temporal vista
represented by a day – in a fury to reach the end
of it, as most people seem to be – one travels at
one's leisure and by easy stages, it is a form of
luxury, a privilege that one cherishes, an aristocratic privilege. For when there is abundant
time for everything, it becomes a matter involving
one's personal dignity that everything should be
done without haste and planned in due sequence.
And although at bottom all Tom's watchful
deliberation, which kept him from ever making a
sudden movement, was caused simply by the
necessity never to lose a beat of that internal
ticking to which he was listening all the time, and
which was merely the non-arrival of the pain that
he dreaded and hoped would never return, the
deliberation of his movements gave him genuine
pleasure, the pleasure of being master both of
them and of such an abundance of time. And
besides, in moving with this controlled slowness
one cancels, one makes merely accidental, the
fact that one could not move more quickly, no
matter how hard one tried. It may have been

this that Mrs. Manson divined when she glanced
at him with that look of alarm.

In the afternoon, if it was fine, they went out
for a short walk. Like everything else that Tom
planned, the hour for setting out was carefully
chosen ; it was the dead time between the dinner rush and the dismissal of the schools, when
very few people were about. Keeping to the
quiet side-streets they would walk slowly along,
conscientiously enjoying their constitutional,
meeting little but an occasional nursemaid push-
a perambulator. At one time Tom could not
have helped casting an appraising glance at these
girls, but now he never even lifted his eyes from
the point on the pavement where the danger
lay ; indeed it seemed beneath his dignity. Still,
there were certain afternoons, afternoons on
which he was more silent than usual, when he did
actually lift his eyes for no more than an instant
to shoot a rancorous glance at the plump
healthy faces of those girls ; and as though his
resentment had been automatically communi-
cated to her too, his mother would make some
indignant and meaningless remark about those
brazen Glasgow hussies. And they would both
walk on sheathed in rancour, a rancour that was
disgust for all that was young and healthy. On
those days they would turn back sooner than
usual, as though they had found an immense
bank of discouragement lying across their path.

Almost every afternoon their road led them
past a school and, looking at the empty concrete
playground, automatically there rose in Tom's
mind, afternoon after afternoon, a memory of a
Sunday walk with his mother long ago which
had taken them past the little country school that
he attended. The playground was of turf and
not of concrete, and in the clear afternoon light
he had peeped in through the gate at the warm,
ragged grass, worn bare in patches and no
longer pounded by the feet of his schoolmates,
but lying lost and vacant ; and he seemed to be
looking at something forbidden. He had glanced
up fearfully at the classroom windows, and his
head felt hot and tight again, as if stuffed with
warm wool ; the feeling one would have if one
were shut in a clothes-cupboard. And he had
run after his mother very fast and taken her hand.
Sometimes he wondered now whether she remembered that walk, but there was nothing in
it for her to remember ; it was like scores of
other walks to her. And at the thought an intense feeling of regret would rise in him ; it
was as though he had lost something which could
never be found again.

For no apparent reason this memory sometimes evoked another, the memory of a young
man, the son of a neighbouring farmer, who had
come home from Edinburgh to die. Tom had
been a mere boy at the time, he could not have

been more than nine, and it had seemed very
strange to him that this young man should have
come home " to die " ; it was as though he had
chosen not only the place and the time, but death
itself, and had returned deliberately to accom-
plish that sad and strange duty. By chance Tom
and his father had met the cart which was bringing the dying man from Blackness to his home ;
he was sitting on a bag stuffed with straw, and
his large, lustrous and very sad eyes were not
looking at the fields and houses he had not seen
for so many years ; he had not looked even at
Tom, although Tom was standing in front of
him on the road, a strange boy that he had never
seen before. And in a few weeks the young man
had died ; and playing in front of the house
Tom had watched the funeral procession winding along the distant road to the churchyard ;
but the sight had not seemed sad, but only very
remote and strange, like the things that happened
in the old ballads his mother sang. Remembering all this now, a blind hunger for the home he
had left swept over him. O God, would he ever
see it again ? Why had he let himself be trapped
here among these miles and miles of houses ?
And he could hardly walk ! He could never
escape by his own strength ; he could never
run away to sea now, even if his mother were
to give him full liberty and bid him go with her
blessing. Why had his father hauled him back

that time? Why had his mother set her face
against his going? They had not known what
they were doing. And while this wave of despair engulfed him he went on planting his feet
carefully on the pavement, kept his eyes fixed
on the point a few steps in front of him, and
listened without losing a beat to the inaudible
ticking on which everything depended. But in
a few minutes he felt very tired, stopped, said
" I'm tired," turned round, and made for home,
anxiously followed by his mother.

This relatively serene interlude lasted almost
for a month. Then, without warning, Tom had
another attack. Coming so unexpectedly and
after such an interval, it threw him into confusion,
his powers were strangely scattered, and it took
him several days to assemble them again. Mrs.
Manson had to implore him to leave his bed,
where he seemed to be hiding. When at last he
reluctantly obeyed, he fell into a deeper pit of
despair, for now he felt palpable difficulty in con-
trolling his limbs, he could no longer conceal it
from himself. What could it mean? What on
earth could it mean? He did not bother even to
shave or put on a collar, but sat by the fire and
only at long intervals lurched to the window to
gaze up at the sky, or to the front room to watch
the people passing in the street. Yet as the days
went by and there was no sign of another attack,
he plucked up courage again, shaved and dressed

himself carefully as before, though a little more
slowly, and even went out now and then in the
afternoon with his mother.

But another attack came, once more unexpectedly, and after that another ; the circle seemed to
be narrowing and narrowing, until, except for
his outings with Mansie in the evenings, its cir-
cumference was the house. For he no longer felt
that it was safe to go out with his mother ; she
could not help him if anything happened ; she
was not strong enough. And anything might
easily happen. For his slowness would no longer
obediently translate itself into a pleasant leisurely
deliberation; it was a palpable defect that he had
to struggle hard to overcome, without being able
to judge, even then, in what measure he had
succeeded. For his sense of time had curiously
changed; it was indeed as though he had two
measures of time now. Everything he did seemed
a little too late. For instance if he stretched out his
hand for the newspaper lying on the table he was
often surprised that his fingers should not reach it
until a quite definite interval had first elapsed ; it
was almost as though he had miscalculated the
distance. And even when he opened his mouth
to say something, the words seemed already said
before he heard, as in a dream, his tongue laboriously and quite unnecessarily repeating them.
Everything he did seemed to be an unnecessary
repetition, retarding him, obstinately delaying

his thoughts before they could move on to something else; or rather everything seemed already done, and all that was left for him was to watch this repetition, this malicious aping of each one of his actions after it had already taken place. And this really frightened him. Suppose when he was out with his mother a boy should run into him! He would be lying on his back before the hand he tried to raise in defence left his side; and he saw himself lying in the street with his hand – too late! – raised against nothing, raised against the sky. A terrible state to be in!

This hiatus in his movements was quite perceptible to anyone who watched him, and if Mansie and Mrs. Manson had not grown accustomed to it very gradually, from its first beginnings, they might have been far more anxious than they were. Jean was the only one who saw clearly the hopelessness of Tom's state, and as the summer wore on she kept more and more to the house in the evenings, seeing Brand only once a week. It was as though she foresaw the end and was silently preparing for it. She said nothing to the others, however; for if they too were to become convinced that Tom would never recover, the house would be unendurable. Yet she was bitterly disappointed by Brand's indifference to Tom's state. They had talked about it one evening, and Brand had pointed out that Tom had always run his head

into things, and that it was asking for trouble to
get off a tramcar in motion when one was drunk.
He had actually used the word " drunk," and
without the least notion that he had been insulting ; on the contrary he had looked to her for
approval, with his triumphant debating air. It
had almost made her sick, and she had flung at
him : " Oh, you're a fool ! " And that had
really penetrated his hide. He had fallen into an
offended silence, and they had parted with few
words.

Yet she had been unfair in reading into Brand's
words a particular indifference to Tom, for he
was indifferent to everything " personal," and
scarcely found any interest even in himself except
for the fact that he was an advocate of Socialism,
a fact of which for some reason he was inordin-
ately vain. And she had been unfair too in feeling insulted by the short and pungent word with
which he had designated Tom's state ; for he
had been thinking in all innocence of nothing but
the most telling way of stating his views, and
the word " drunk " had in the context an artistic
and logical appositeness which, even if he had
divined Jean's susceptibilities, he would have
found it hard to forgo ; it would have been like
a violation of his æsthetic sense of fitness. But
so intent was he on the general question that he
had never thought of her feelings at all. Besides,
she had deliberately introduced a personal

matter, had wantonly embarked on the kind of
talk that he called gossip, and that it was gossip
about dying made it only the more inexcusable.
For death was one of those questions which did
not interest him even in their general aspect,
seeing that it could never be solved and so to
think of it at all was a wasteful expense of time.
" I'm only concerned with evils that can be
remedied," he was fond of saying whenever
any of those metaphysical problems which trouble
even the most ignorant of mankind were brought
up. And he would glance round him with a look
of conscious rightness, asking for approval like
a bright child repeating an incontestable maxim.

None the less, Mansie's coldness and Jean's
outburst of contemptuous anger shook him. He
felt at a loss in this atmosphere where the personal had unaccountably grown to such dimensions, overshadowing and bleaching all colour
out of the general, and making even the
most clinching argument hollow and unreal.
Jean listened to him still, but as she listened he
could feel his authenticity oozing out of him,
could feel himself, a militant Socialist, fading to
an almost transparent insignificance, so that
when he sat in the kitchen with Mrs. Manson and
Jean and Mansie and Tom, sometimes he could
hardly convince himself that he was there, no
matter how hard he talked. Nor indeed was he
actually there to them except as a troubling

succession of words, a sequence of syllables in an imperfectly known foreign tongue which one followed with difficulty, or was content – for it did not really matter – not to follow at all. So it was no wonder that in pained perplexity Brand should at last cease to visit the house, and fall back on his weekly meeting with Jean. And no sooner was he gone than he was forgotten ; and if once in a few weeks someone said with a surprised air, " David Brand hasn't been in for a long time," the words were as empty either of relief or regret as a newspaper paragraph containing a piece of unimportant news from a distant country. It was as though he had faded to such complete nonentity before the reality which preoccupied the household that the removal of his visible presence made no difference, created no void. And indeed in his last visits he had become – an unprecedented experience for him – almost silent as well as null.

17

THEY walked along the still canal. The sun had set long since, but the light was still ebbing. As it faded it became more and more transparent, so that what was left was not darkness, the darkness that the eyes expected and almost longed for, but an unearthly stationary clarity into which every object rose distinctly but blindly, as though already coiled in sleep within itself and turned away from all that was round it. The water in the canal shone like polished steel; it shone blankly, as though nothing but itself were there. In front, quite far away, another pair of lovers were walking with their arms round each other. Nobody else was in sight. It was midsummer.

"He's been queer since the last attack," said Mansie. It was always at this hour, when the light was fading and their faces were turned towards Glasgow again, that they talked about Tom. They never mentioned him by name.

Mansie had taken his arm from Helen's waist when he began to speak about his brother. The pair away in front were still walking with their arms round each other.

Helen looked at him but made no reply. Mansie walked on for a little, then he said : " He seems to be thinking of something all the time. I've done my best to rouse his interest, but it's no use."

" Maybe he'll come round by himself," said Helen. " He was always moody."

Mansie was silent again. Then he said : " Yes, he may come round by himself. I wish I understood him. But he never tells me anything. He goes his own road, as he's always done. I've never known all my life what he would be up to next. He was always reckless."

" Yes, he was terribly reckless. Sometimes I've almost been afraid of him, Mansie."

Mansie frowned as though the words displeased him and said : " He's never hurt anybody but himself." Then after a pause : " It was hard lines that this should come just when the fellow had turned over a new leaf." And after another pause : " He's greatly changed."

Helen made no reply. The darkness was now falling at last ; one could no longer see whether the two in front had their arms round each other.

As if encouraged by the darkness, Mansie said presently, speaking into it as one speaks into an unlighted room knowing that someone else is there : " Well, there's this comfort : when he recovers he'll be a different fellow."

And Helen's voice answered cheerfully at

his side : " Yes, and then everything will be for the best after all."

The confidence in her voice made him uneasy for some reason, but there was nothing more to be said. And when they had gone on for a little farther in silence he put his arm round Helen's waist again. It was a reassurance.

18

Und die findigen Tiere merken es schon
dass wir nicht sehr verlässlich zu Haus sind
in der gedeuteten Welt.

RAINER MARIA RILKE

WHEN he was twelve Mansie had had a curious experience. It took up only a few minutes, but afterwards it seemed to have filled the whole of that summer afternoon, and to have coloured not only the hours which followed, but the preceding hour as well, which became a mysterious time of preparation whose warnings he had not heeded.

" That strange afternoon " was how he thought of it, and the strangeness had begun with the class being dismissed after the dinner hour. Some state event had just been published, an important event, for it had to do with the royal family, yet human and touching, for it might have happened in any ordinary household; and this perhaps was what had made the teacher's voice, for all its reverence, sound almost confidential when he asked the class to give three cheers. Yet there had been something unreal in

the teacher's elation, and although the class were
glad to get such an unlooked-for holiday, and
felt grateful to the royal family, the three cheers
had a hypocritical ring. Afterwards Mansie's
companions had decided to spend the afternoon
in town, and he had taken the road alone. In the
bright afternoon sun the road looked unusually
deserted; on the fields the men and women
seemed more active than usual, as though they
had just begun the day's work, a day in which
time had been displaced in some curious way,
making everything both too early and too late.
So even the wild flowers along the roadside were
unfamiliar, as though they had sprung up that
moment, supplanting the ones that should have
been there. Still, this was the road he had always
taken, and so he went on.

It was in the little sunken field sloping down
to the burn that it happened. There were
generally several horses in this field, and he had
always passed them without thinking. This day,
however – it may have been because of the dis-
placement of everything, for the shifting of time
had subtly redistributed the objects scattered over
space as well – there was only one horse, a young
dark chestnut with a white star on its brow.
Mansie had almost reached the footbridge over
the burn before he saw it, for it was standing
half-hidden in a clump of bushes. They caught
sight of each other at the same moment, and

Mansie stopped as though a hand had been laid on his forehead : into his mind came instantaneously, as a final statement of something, the words : "A boy and a horse." For out of the bushes the horse looked at him with a scrutiny so devouring and yet remote that it seemed to isolate him, to enclose him completely in the moment and in himself, making him a boy without a name standing in a field ; yet this instantaneous act of recognition came from a creature so strange to him that he felt some unimaginable disaster must break in if he did not tear his eyes away. This feeling was so strong that his body seemed to grow hollow. Then slowly the stone dyke by which he had stopped grew up, wavered, and steadied itself ; he put out his hand to it, the stones were rough and warm, and this gave him courage to stand his ground a little longer. But now as he gazed on at the horse, which still stared steadily and fiercely at him, he seemed on the point of falling into another abyss, not of terror this time, but of pure strangeness. For unimaginable things radiated from the horse's eyes ; it seemed to be looking at him from another world which lay like a hidden kingdom round it, and in that world it might be anything ; and a phrase from a school book, " the kingly judge," came into his mind. And how could he tell what it might do to him ? It might trample him to death or lift him up by its teeth and bear

him away to that other world. He took to his
heels and did not feel safe until he was at the other
side of the footbridge, with the burn behind him.

At the time Mansie was not of course aware
of all those feelings ; he was merely filled with
terror of something very strange, and felt –
though this perhaps was a deliberate fancy – that
if he had waited a moment longer the horse might
have carried out its sentence on him. But when,
several months later, he happened to look at a
portrait of John Knox in *The Scots Worthies*, the
long face, still more elongated by the wiry, animal-
looking beard, transported him to that field
again, and he felt afraid of the eyes gazing out at
him from the flat smooth page. And one day in
Glasgow many years later he caught sight of a
plaster statue in a shop window and suddenly
felt dizzy, standing on the hot pavement ; and
although a tramcar clanked past, throwing sharp
beams from its windows into the dark window of
the shop, he again felt transported to that distant
hot still field, and the sound made by a message-
boy running past echoed in his ears like the sound
of his own feet on the little footbridge. Strange !
he had clean forgotten that afternoon. In a little
he saw that there were two names outlined in
rough relief at the foot of the plaster cast :
"Moses" and in smaller letters "Michelangelo."
Michelangelo was a great man ; the Reverend
John often mentioned him in his sermons. Queer

how solid the beard looked, just as solid as the
head, all of a piece like the head of some strange
animal, and the two funny little horns on the
forehead were like blunt pricked ears. Uncanny,
the thoughts that must have been in the mind of
the fellow who made that thing. And yet the
Reverend John thought a lot of him, so he must
have been a Christian ; all the same one simply
couldn't think of a Christian bringing out a
thing like that. Almost frightening ! And
later, when he picked up *Gulliver's Travels* one
evening in Brand's lodgings, the book fell open
at a very queer picture, " The King of the
Hou——" something or other, it was called,
and it showed a horse sitting on a throne with
a crowd of naked shivering people before it.
Mansie could not take his eyes off it. The
horse's front hoofs drooped clumsily and helplessly from the legs outstretched like iron bars ;
but the massive haunches, too heavy for the frail
throne on which they rested, were powerful and
majestic in spite of the curly and somewhat mean
legs in which they ended. A queer picture ; if
he hadn't been ashamed of exposing his ignorance
he would have asked Brand about it. And later
still, when the Reverend John gave a sermon on
the Pharaohs, there rose in Mansie's mind, a
little obscenely, a picture of those powerful
wrinkled haunches and that long, austere and
somewhat stupid skull, so hard that it seemed to

be made of granite rather than bone. If *that* were set on a throne of justice, by gum you would have to sit up! Not much friendliness about justice of that kind. Made a fellow shiver when he thought of it. Seemed to take all the stuffing out of a fellow.

The autumn holiday had come; Tom did not yet show the hoped-for improvement; so there was no possibility of Mansie's getting away for the week-end. But on Sunday, as Tom said that he intended to remain in the house, Mansie resolved to take a walk in the country. As he shaved he went over in his mind all his acquaintances; every single one of them away, he decided bitterly; of course one could hardly expect them to stay in Glasgow simply because—— But still it rather let a fellow down. In morose resignation he took the tramcar to Killermont, pleased that there should be hardly anyone in it but himself; yes, they were all away at Rothesay or Dunoon or Helensburgh, and it was right that the other passengers in the tramcar should look ashamed and furtive; all except the conductor, of course, who had a right to be there. Still, the fellow showed his contempt for them a little too plainly when he shouted jokes from one end of the almost empty tramcar to the other, as if only he and the driver were there. Like these Glasgow keelies.

But when, having walked through Bearsden,

Mansie turned into the footpath over the gentle
hilly grasslands leading to Strathblane, his spirits
began to rise; perhaps after all he would meet
some solitary rambler from the Clarion Scouts;
somebody would be sure to be on the road. He
would have a rest when he came to Craigallion.
But when he approached the gate leading into
the field where the pretty little sylvan loch lay
among its half-ring of trees, he stopped short, for
a young horse was standing behind the gate
watching him. Everything grew still and bright,
the long grasses by the roadside became quite
motionless, and the wooden bars of the gate
looked all at once so solid that no effort could
ever prevail against them; they ran smoothly
from side to side of the gate like a goal which
one might touch, but never pass. No, he could
never go through that gate. And suddenly,
staring at the chestnut horse standing behind it
Mansie thought, and it was as though an oracle
or a Pharaoh had spoken : " Tom will die." The
shock of the thought made him feel a little dizzy ;
he looked across at the bald crown of Dum-
goyne : it was very bare, he had never realised
before that it was so bare. So far away too, and
this gate and this horse were so near. Why was
one thing in one place and another in another?
A complete riddle, the way things were scattered
about on the face of the earth, hills and houses
and rocks and gates and horses. Why shouldn't

the hill be here and the gate and the horse somewhere else, in some peaceful distant place ? And
what was a hill anyway ? A clumsy big thing
without conceivable use to anybody. Yes, it
was ridiculous that a horse should be standing
beside a gate. Things were just dumped down
anywhere and anyhow ; you had literally to pick
your way among them, to walk round them and
be very careful even then, for you couldn't even
be sure that they would stay in the same place ;
lots of them moved, and some of them rushed
about at a great speed, tramcars and things like
that, and at times, in spite of all the space in the
world, they banged straight into one another.
If a horse like that were to let fly at you with its
hind hoofs you would just curl up.

With a rush of relief he realised that he need
not go through that field, need not pass through
that gate, for the road he was standing on would
take him by a roundabout way to Strathblane :
you could get to places after all if you made up
your mind ! And as he walked on, not once turning his head to look back at the horse, he felt as
though he had circumvented Fate and perhaps
done Tom a good turn he would never know of.
But presently the refrain returned again : " Tom
will die. Tom will die." It was outrageous to
be pursued by such thoughts ; besides they didn't
seem to be his at all, they didn't seem real. They
were like something you read about ; why, maybe

this was what people meant by poetry? And once
more he felt relieved, for poetry wasn't real life;
it was imagination. Yet it was strange this had
never happened to him before, there was something dashed funny about it, and he tentatively
tried the words over again; they didn't commit
him to anything. "Tom will die. Tom will
die": the refrain beat on, filling his ears as he
walked on slowly amid the brightness and
silence. Then quite unexpectedly the hills
trembled and dissolved; tears were running
down his cheeks. Yes, he knew it now! Tom
would die! And he gave himself over to his
grief, seized upon it as though it were a precious
draught he had long been waiting for and must
drink to the end lest it might never return again;
and he let the tears flow and when they showed
signs of stopping started them afresh with the
hypnotic beat of the refrain: "Tom will die.
Tom will die." What was he doing? It was
almost like an act of treachery to his brother!
Yet his tears were not real tears, they didn't
count, they didn't mean that Tom would really
die. What on earth could they mean?

The fit passed. He washed his face in a little
wayside stream, washed it shamelessly and matter-
of-factly as one might wash one's hands after a
dirty but necessary job. Yet when he thought of
Tom now everything seemed more hopeful. He
felt better, and he was convinced that Tom was

better too, that Tom had at last improved, perhaps since that morning.

Turning the corner he came upon a pale milky-
faced little man in rusty blue serge, who was
bending over some weeds by the wayside. It
was Geordie Henderson, and when he looked up
and nodded Mansie was almost sorry for once
to meet someone he knew. A nice fellow
Geordie, of course, a kind soul in spite of the way
he liked to talk about frogs and the survival of
the fittest and the freezing-out of the whole
human race in a few million years. Still Mansie's
heart sank when he saw the soft pale milky face,
a face so pervasively milky that even the blue of
the eyes had the opaqueness of soap-suds. And
pitilessly ignoring Geordie's welcoming look he
walked on with a curt " Nice day." Everything
seemed to be scattered in confusion again like
boulders on a vast plain. That dashed horse !
And Henderson with his invertebrates and his
amœbas and his protoplasm ! What use were
such words to a fellow ? And Geordie's milki-
ness seemed to shrivel into small dry grains, like
the new kind of milk that was sold in tins : dried
milk, they called it. That was all Henderson was,
just dried milk.

And Mansie remembered a Sunday ramble with
Geordie. In the middle of a field where cows
were grazing they had come upon a huge rock
six feet high. The rock looked funny enough

there in all conscience, but when Geordie began
to talk learnedly of how it could have got there,
that was surely making too great a song about it.
The rock had been carried there, Geordie decided, by an ice block that slid across Europe at
the end of a glacial period. That was science, of
course, and Mansie had listened respectfully, but
at the same time he couldn't help thinking : All
very well to blether about this rock, but, when it
comes to the point, how did anything get where it
is ?   And on the top of this recollection he remembered the feelings he had had when his father
removed from the farm in the island to the one
near Blackness.   Yes, he had felt just the same
then looking at the new countryside – though he
had clean forgotten about it : that everything
was a little out of position, that things needn't
have been as they were at all.   The sea needn't
have swept in just there, the hills needn't have
been just that shape ; and the same with the farm-
houses : they were set down just anywhere, and
one of them was planted in a position that it
made you uncomfortable even to look at : it
was about two-thirds up the side of a hill, when
of course it should have been either at the top
or the bottom.   But then he had got accustomed
to all those things, and in time it seemed quite
natural that they should be as they were and where
they were.   They seemed at last even to have a
sort of plan ; yet if he were to go back now and

look at them again he would find that that was
pure fancy. Still it was a dashed uncomfortable
thought. Made a fellow wonder where he was.

Terrible to think too of those millions of years
stretching in front, for what with things moving
about as they did and even taking different
shapes (according to Geordie), how on earth
could a fellow know where he was ? Even those
historical Johnnies that they taught you about at
school, Cromwell and Henry the Eighth and
Napoleon and so on, would never be able to
stick to their places for good ; they would all
have to shift, no matter how hard they fought
against it. In a million years they might be anywhere, out of history altogether maybe, for how
could the schools go on teaching history as far
back as that ? Everything on the earth now
would be forgotten, things changed so fast.
Maybe even Christianity would be forgotten,
perhaps even Christ Himself, or at least He
might become one of those nature myths Geordie
was always blethering about. Even that was possible. And then there were earthquakes to be
taken into account ; always something else when
you thought you had provided for everything.
Suppose Palestine were to subside and be covered by the sea ? That was quite possible. And
he saw on the sunken reef of Calvary a luminous
Cross covered with jewelled sea creatures and
glimmering phosphorescently in dark blue waters.

A phrase he had heard somewhere, " sea gods," came into his mind. Would Christ become a sea god then instead of a nature myth? And he saw fleets of submarines circling round the silver-dripping Cross, fleets filled with strange-faced pilgrims from a distant age : worshippers of the amphibious god. Queer thoughts that came into a fellow's head. Well, he wouldn't like to be the last Johnny left to be frozen out. At the thought he almost felt inclined to turn back and seek Geordie's company.

When he reached the tea-room in Strathblane he was glad to find the tables crowded, glad that he had to sit down at a table where two young men were eating. And when he ventured a " Lovely day " he was grateful that the two young men said something friendly in return, for he had a sense of having come back from such a vast and watery distance that the very look on his face, the very air he carried with him, might well scare any decent fellow. He basked in the friendly over-crowded atmosphere of the tea-room, drank in like an immaterial refreshment the jokes flying about, almost reverently masticated the thick floury buttered scones, as though they were friendly and helpful substances humbly offering themselves to him, voluntarily sacrificing themselves to prove that the earth was a great and kindly living thing and not a plain of boulders and rocks.

Comforted, he went out into the garden, sat down in a deck-chair, and lit a cigarette. For a long time he lay in a dense cloud of animal comfort, his mind blank. The crystalline evening light fell in a calm and frozen cataract on the little garden, the thick rhododendron leaves rose into it rigid and shining, the roses gleamed lustrously as though wet with spray. Steadily the slanting cataract fell, but on the uplands to the east, on the high level fields, its fall quickened to a race of light, a wind of pale fire flying over the sward, which it turned golden as it ran onwards to the invisible walls and roofs of Glasgow. There too it would bring radiance and peace, and even if there were some house of sickness or pain there, it too would be drowned in that serenity; the little stubborn point of pain must dissolve in shame amid such peace. It was like paradise. All this talk about natural selection and proto-plasm didn't seem very real now. Dried milk. He got up, said good night to the waitress, and set out.

He climbed the slope to the gate of the field in which lay the little loch. He looked up; he could scarcely believe his eyes: that dashed horse was at *this* gate now! Could he never get away from it? He walked straight up to the gate; he looked for a moment deep into the white star in the middle of the horse's brow; it was remote and pure as a planet in the sky, and it gave him a queasy feeling at the pit of his stomach. Then he lifted his walking-stick and said in a quivering voice : " Get out, damn you ! Get out of this ! " He swung his stick, the horse tossed its head, shied, turned round, and, flinging up its hind hoofs, slowly trotted away. Mansie climbed over the gate with his legs trembling. The horse was not far enough away yet for his taste, so he picked up a stone and walked towards it. " Get out ! " he shouted again, making to fling the stone, but now the horse finally cantered away quite casually without looking at him. Mansie felt very tired ; yet he walked on rapidly without looking to right or left, took his way mechanically through gates and down lanes and round corners, until he found himself at Killermont, where a lighted tramcar was waiting. This business of Tom's might turn out to be serious, he kept thinking. Have to see whether anything can be done. Maybe a special-ist should be called in. He longed for Wednes-day, so that he might talk with Helen about it, for he saw in a flash that she alone could help him. He hurried home almost in a panic. But Tom was neither better nor worse. He had had a quiet day.

19

Warum ? Wofür ? Wodurch ? Wohin ? Wo ? Wie ?

NIETZSCHE

A MAN of our time who is converted from a Christian creed to one of the modern faiths takes without knowing it several centuries at one leap. He launches himself out of a world in which the church bells are still ringing, reminding him of the brevity of his life and the need for salvation, and in the twinkling of an eye he is standing in a landscape from which thousand-year-old lights and shadows have been wiped clean away, a shadowless landscape where every object is new, bright, pure and naked ; and while he is contemplating it the medieval bells, still ringing, die away to a thin, antiquarian jangle in his ears. The astonishing thing is that he should be able to execute this feat without becoming dizzy. Yet often it is accomplished with trance-like ease, as though he were flying ; and that is because during the brief time he is in the air he has been metamorphosed with chemical rapidity and thoroughness, and so it is a new man, perfectly adapted to

his new surroundings, who lands at his mark.
He has experienced a change of heart. And
although between the creed, say, of a Baptist,
the most narrowly individualistic of all creeds,
and that of a Socialist, which is communistic
through and through, there lies the gulf between
the religious and the secular, as well as several
centuries of human thought, the convert behaves
in the most natural manner as though he were
merely stepping out of one room into another
furnished more to his taste.

The difference between the world he has left
and the one he enters now is perhaps simply the
difference between Why and How. And perhaps
he has had no choice. For if a man lives in a large
modern city where existence is insecure, and change
is rapid, and further change imperative; where
chaos is a standing threat, and yet in the refluent
ballet of becoming every optimistic idea seems on
tip-toe to be realised; where at the very lowest
one must put one's best foot forward to keep up
with the march of invention and innovation:
the How challenges at every turn and one is
irresistibly driven into its arms. Once there,
however, one finds that the Why has become an
importunate and niggardly claim, holding one
back; and so without scruple, indeed with a
sense of following the deepest dictates of conscience, one casts it off, and with it apparently
all concern for the brevity of one's life, the

immortality of one's soul, salvation, and God.
Strange how easily all this can be done!

To fulfil itself the Why must conduct us to the
definite end of its seeking; but the How leads
on and on through the endless mutations of
endless appearance, as if it were set upon cir-
cumnavigating a world into which one dimension
too many has entered, so that it can never
completely describe its circle. Nevertheless the
How goes on striving towards horizon after
horizon, each of which, like a door, merely
throws open another circular chamber, and after
that another, and after that another; it casts
horizon after horizon behind it like great spent
coins, interesting now only to the antiquarian.
At first the convert finds nothing but delight in
the potentialities of this new world where he can
lose himself a thousand times and always find
himself again; but as time goes on infinity
itself, which seemed the most imponderable of
things, begins to weigh upon him like a massive
vault, walling and roofing him in; and though
it surrounds him at an inimaginable distance,
sometimes it seems uncomfortably immediate,
for after all there is nothing very substantial
between it and him, and so he may run slap into
it one day at the corner of a street, although it
appeared to be millions and millions of miles
away.

To run slap into infinity is a momentarily

annihilating experience ; a man who chances to
do it no longer knows where he is and cannot
account even for the simplest objects round him.
Quite irrational questions spring up : " How
am I here ? Why is this thing in this place and
that thing in that ? Why does one moment come
before or after another ? Am I really here ?
Am I at all ? " And he hastens to put something
between him and an infinity that is annulling him,
something so vast that it will fill all space and
time and, leave no gap anywhere for that dreadful
hiatus, that mad blank like the abyss between two
breaths one of which may never be drawn – that
hole into which he and all things may fall and
never be found again. He seeks a How that will
fill the cosmos, a How so great that it almost
seems a Why : he embraces the universal process
itself, although, accepting the jargon of his age,
he may merely call it evolution.

People of traditional religious feeling are
mystified and repelled by such terms as the
religion of humanity, the religion of science, the
religion of evolution. They cannot understand
how anyone can put personal faith in the universe,
call upon it for personal aid, and look towards it
for personal salvation ; and to do so seems to
them not only blasphemous, but also simple-
minded. Yet such a thing is easy to comprehend,
and that simply because once man has fashioned
a How of cosmic proportions it reinstates in his

mind the problems, the very terms, of religion.
He broods once more over immortality, though
it may be merely the provisional immortality of
humanity's linked generations ; and he recognises
the need for salvation, even if by that he means
nothing more than the secular consummation of
human hopes. Heaven itself, removed from
eternity, which has become void, indeed non-
existent, appears again as an infinitely distant
dream of the earth's future, a dream so deep that
the shadows of sin and death have almost vanished into it, have been almost, but not quite,
dreamt away. Nor is the dogma of grace
definitely abolished ; for the almost providential
appearance of the saving How rescues the
believer, if not from damnation, at least from
imminent absorption by a blank cosmos, and he
reposes in the universal process as the Christian
reposes in God.

So it is quite understandable that the emotions
with which he contemplates this How should be
religious emotions, or at least should run so
exactly parallel to their counterparts that a fallible
human being may easily confound them, or even
hold that *this* is the true and *that* the false. And
this is what generally happens at the beginning,
until the hour of doubt, which every genuine
faith has to surmount, somewhat blankly strikes.
Then there may fall on the believer a fear which
the How, in spite of all its majestic inclusiveness,

is impotent to relieve. And it is not merely the fear that can be caused by the recognition that this How, this pseudo-Why, is itself in process of changing, so that one has none but shifting ground beneath one's feet – for one can get accustomed to that sensation and even acquire a liking for it which may last for the years of a man's life : no, it is a far deeper and yet vacant fear, the fear that if one were to comprehend the How from beginning to end, seeing every point in the universal future as luminously as the momentary and local point at which one stands, and seeing oneself with the same clarity as part of that whole, the universe might turn out to be merely a gigantic crystalline machine before which one must stand in blank contemplation, incapable any longer even of looking for a Why in it, so finally, though inexplicably, would that one thing be excluded by the consummated How. A man who has realised this fear, yet who longs for a faith that shall transfigure life, will be betrayed into a final mad affirmation, and in the vision of the Eternal Recurrence will summon from the void a blind and halt eternity to provide a little cheer and society for blind and halt time, and so alleviate its intolerable pathos.

It is a fear such as this that sometimes hovers round Socialistic dreams of the future. Like the visions of the saints, the Socialist vision is one of purification, and arises from man's need to rid himself of his uncleanness, the effluvia of his body and the dark thoughts of his mind. Yet the Socialist does not get rid of them in the fires of death, from which the soul issues cleansed and transfigured, but rather by a painless vaporisation of all that is urgent and painful in a future which is just as earthly as the present. The purity of the figures in his vision is accordingly the purity of, the elements, of the sea and the winds, of air and fire, perhaps in rare moments of a scented flowering tree ; it is a chemical or bio-chemical purity, not a spiritual. It is what is left when man eliminates from himself all that is displeasing, unclean and painful ; and that residue is finally the mere human semblance, deprived of all attributes save two, shape and colour : a beautiful pallid abstract of the human form. Yet it might still be a negative vision of perfection if it were not for one thing, that the dreamer is unable to think away from all those multitudes of lovely beings death and dissolution ; and as mortality never seems more dreadful than when it is beauty that it consumes, the more radiant the vision of a transfigured humanity becomes, the more deeply it is tinged with fear. Until something, perhaps the dread of death for one he knows, opens the dreamer's eyes, and he sees that all those future generations of whom he has thought are only ordinary human beings without entrails. And with that his vision of the very earth upon which they walk is disastrously and yet beautifully changed; it is a world of glittering rocks and flowers, of towering pinnacled rocks and waving hills of empty blossoms: a barren world, for without the digestive tract and the excretary canal how could there be flourishing orchards and fields yellow with corn?

Yet this dream teases him persistently, for it need change only once more, he thinks, and it might after all become the beatific vision. But when it does change something very different is left him – an empty world, the symbol and precursor of that which will come when all life has been frozen from it. And it seems to him that his vision has been made of the wrong substance, and he begins to divine why over it the shadows of fear and mortality should fall so heavily, far more heavily than in the indeterminate light of his own days.

20

Qu'as-tu fait, O toi que voilà
  Pleurant sans cesse,
Dis, qu'as-tu fait, toi que voilà
  De ta jeunesse ?

VERLAINE

AFTER all Mansie did not speak to Helen about Tom's state when he met her next Wednesday evening, and several weeks passed without anything happening. Then one night Tom had a very severe stroke. When he awoke late next morning the pain was gone, but for a while he did not seem to know where he was. He stayed in bed all day, ate the food his mother gave him, but when she asked whether he felt better only stared gloomily at her without replying.

His gloom still lasted in the evening when Mansie returned. Mansie sat down at the table to his kippers and tea. A fellow had to eat whatever happened. After he had finished he went over to the bed: " Come, Tom, buck up. . . . Would you like to see the doctor ? "

Tom replied : " I won't see any doctor. It's all up. I'm done for."

Mansie glanced in alarm behind him. Thank God, his mother wasn't in the room. Well, this settled it ; a specialist would have to be called in now. He had been quite right that evening after all, walking back from Strathblane. He said, but his words sounded empty, like words cheerfully spoken when everything is over : " I tell you what, Tom, we'll go along and see a specialist. It's my opinion that this doctor fellow doesn't know what he's talking about. There's a professor in the Western Infirmary, Bob says, that knows more about a fellow's head than anybody else in the United Kingdom."

" All right, fix an appointment with your specialist if you like," said Tom glumly. But in a few minutes he became more cheerful, and when Mansie returned next evening he was clothed and sitting expectantly by the fire.

" I've fixed it up," said Mansie, " Friday afternoon at three."

A flush overspread Tom's face and quite slowly faded again, leaving him very pale.

" Nothing to get anxious about," said Mansie. " Just like a visit to an ordinary doctor. Only that this fellow knows what he's talking about."

Presently Mrs. Manson came in and was told the news, and at her exclamations of delight they all became gay and even Tom forgot his watchful gravity. But when in a little while he got to his feet to walk out of the room, all his gloom fell

back upon him again. For he was feeling damned
unsteady on his pins to-day, far worse than he
could remember ever having felt before ; no use
trying to hide the fact. Mansie was sitting beside
the window. Whatever was Tom up to ? Why
was he doing that with his legs ? Pretending to
be drunk, or what ? And a purely automatic
smile appeared on Mansie's face ; it was so dashed
funny, the way Tom made one leg waggle while
the other was quite steady ! Mansie came to
himself : Why, the fellow was far worse than
yesterday ! And he was about to get to his feet
when suddenly Tom turned to Mrs. Manson and
said : " He's sitting there laughing at me ! And
I can hardly walk ! " Mansie started from his
chair as though it were a place of shame :

" No, no, Tom, I wasn't laughing ! I swear
to God I wasn't."

" You were. I saw you," said Tom sternly.
Then, as if that question were settled, he went on :
" Lend a hand here. I need to go to the water-
closet."

Mansie put his hand under Tom's left elbow
and helped him across the lobby. Tom's body
felt curiously soft and jointless. They pushed
their way clumsily through the narrow door of the
water-closet, their feet making a loud scuffling
noise on the linoleum. Mansie turned to go.
" Stop here," said Tom, like a master speaking to
a servant. Mansie stood leaning against the wall

of the narrow little room with his eyes on the floor.

But when Tom turned round presently Mansie was surprised to see his face all blubbered with tears.

"I've wasted my whole life, Mansie," he said, and it was as if he had decoyed Mansie here by a childish stratagem for this confession. "I've made a complete mess of it. And now I'm done for." His red unshaven chin quivered like an old woman's, and with trembling hands he tried to fasten the buttons on the front of his trousers, but then let his arms fall helplessly by his side. Mansie looked over his shoulder at the backs of the houses opposite. He kept his eyes fixed out there, so that some part of him at least might be out of this cell where he was standing with his brother. He answered in a deliberately careless voice: "No, no, Tom, that's all nonsense."

But Tom went on steadily as though he were preparing for a long and serious talk, during which even the buttoning of his trousers could wait; though that omission evidently troubled him, for his hands kept wandering to his buttons, but without closing with them. Perhaps what had started him was simply a confused sense that this room was the one in the house best suited for heart to heart masculine confession, for talking freely without any risk of being interrupted by the women; perhaps a vague memory of maudlin

confidences to tipsy friends in the privacy of
public-house urinals had risen without his knowledge to his mind. At any rate he went on :
" It's the God's truth, Mansie. I know what I'm
talking about. I might have gone to the Colonies
and made good long ago. Might have had a
wife and kids by this time. A home of my own.
God, what a mess I've made of my life. And
now——" But there, when he seemed to be
well set, he broke off with a sob and tried again
to fasten the buttons of his trousers, but once
more helplessly let his arms fall.

Unendurable pity rose up in Mansie. " Here,
Tom," he said, and he bent down hastily and
fastened the buttons. Then he put his arm under
Tom's ; " And don't say you're done for !
Remember we're going to the specialist on
Friday. Dash it, it isn't your fault that you're
ill ! You'll be all right again soon."

Tom dried his tears, and they returned to the
kitchen.

But now Mansie had to hurry away to keep his
appointment with Helen. And such a mechanical thing is habit that he did so almost as though
he were going to an ordinary assignation. But
as he sat in the tramcar, suddenly he felt that
something extraordinary must happen. As if
that confession in the water-closet, that prison
confession, had united him to Tom as they had
never been united before, he felt in his own body

that Tom was dying, felt death in his own flesh, and it was almost with a dying man's eyes that he saw Helen now. What did she matter? Tom was a complete wreck; helpless as a child. His younger brother. And she had flung his hair into the sea, and he, Mansie Manson, had looked on and said nothing. What could have come over him? What could have made him do a thing like that? Worse even than smiling at Tom's helplessness. How could he have done that either? He hadn't meant to, but how could even his face have smiled? Couldn't trust even yourself, it seemed. A terrible position for a fellow to have got into between that girl and his brother. Oh well, everything was smashed up now. Tom was dying, and if he died he would be between them all the rest of their lives. Mansie's heart contracted and seemed to grow very small. They would have to give each other up, never see each other again. It seemed a for-tuitous thought, and it was with astonishment that he suddenly saw: that was really how things stood! Oh, why was Tom dying on them like this? But the cry seemed to be dead before it rose; it was a purely hypothetical cry, enveloped in layer after layer of impotence like the struggles of a patient under an anæsthetic. He felt wooden and stupid. What was the use of feeling when everything was smashed to pieces?

Helen was waiting for him at Eglinton Toll.

At the sight of his pale face she hurried forward
anxiously and asked : " What's wrong, Mansie ?
Are you ill ? " He saw the mouth and eyes he
had kissed so often and they seemed so natural,
so intimate, so inevitable, like a permanent part
of his world, that his limbs lost their wooden-
ness, he became again the Mansie who had
stepped on to this pavement so often before and
looked at that mouth and those eyes, and there
seemed no reason why he and Helen should not
have their walk as if this were any other evening,
no reason why they should not simply go on
having their walks indefinitely. But then she
asked in the expressionless tone into which she
fell whenever she spoke of Tom : " Has he had
another attack ? " And Mansie's limbs became
wooden again, and he said woodenly : " Yes."
Then he added : " I must go back to him at
once." He had not intended to say this, and he
was a little scared at his own words ; but suddenly it was all unbearable : the tram ride to
Maxwell Park, and the weary walk with Helen
through the dark or lamp-lit roads. No, he
couldn't talk about Tom to her if she was to speak
in that terrible voice. He would write.

" If he's ill," said Helen, still in the same voice,
looking away, " of course you must go back to
him."

Oh, why couldn't she call him Tom for once !
He was his brother, after all !

" I'll write," he said. Then he was silent
again. There seemed nothing to say. But then,
as if he were remembering a piece of news that
he had overlooked, he went on : " He's to see a
specialist on Friday." Now there was nothing at
all left to say, so he said : " I think he's dying."

" No, no, Mansie, you can't mean that ! " she
cried as though he had tried to wound her.

" I'm almost certain of it," he said stubbornly.
Was it his fault if Tom was dying ?

" But I never thought – I never thought——"
her words died, she looked at him as if for help,
and then glanced away.

People and cars were passing. What was the
use of standing here ? And to put an end to the
unbearable silence he said : " I don't know what's
going to happen after this. I'll write," and without his being able to help it there was a threat
now in the words. His heart, as he stood there,
seemed to be hardening by a perfectly arbitrary
process over which he had no control ; he could
do nothing but stand and let it grow harder and
harder. It seemed a pity for her, certainly ; he
felt sorry for her, but he could find nothing to
say. No use.

" Good night," he said. He took her hand,
which was cold and nerveless, and let it fall
again. It seemed a wanton act of cruelty – his
hand was so hard, and hers so soft and defenceless. Well, he hadn't meant to hurt her. He said

again : " I'll write," raised his hat and turned away and left her standing at the corner.

That was over. He felt very tired. He might as well go home.

21

THEY descended the steps before the hospital and walked along the red gravel path towards the cab that was waiting for them. Presently Tom asked without lifting his eyes:

" What did he say ? "

The specialist's words were running in Mansie's head : " I can do nothing. It may be a matter of months, possibly of weeks." Mansie cleared his throat : " He says you're just to go on . . . just go on quietly," then he took the plunge, " and it will get better in time."

Tom listened with his head to one side as if weighing Mansie's words, but he did not look up, and even when they were sitting in the cab they still avoided looking at each other.

" Go on quietly ! " Tom said at last to the floor of the cab. " Is that all he said ? It's easy for him to talk ! "

Mansie gazed out through the window at the sooty front-garden railings spinning past. It was a dull November afternoon. Why had he said that about going on quietly ? A child could see through it, and he was astonished and a little shocked that

Tom hadn't. But Tom was really as helpless as a child, couldn't even fasten his buttons. He replied with an effort: "Oh, he said you weren't to worry. That's the only thing that might do harm."

It was as though he were talking to an object that had Tom's shape and was able to reply in Tom's voice, but that was all : an object that you carted about in a cab and had to deliver like a package at its destination. It didn't matter what one said now, and yet it was hard work to say anything at all. Tom asked :

" Did he say how long it would take ? "

And mechanically Mansie responded : " He said it might be a matter of months, but possibly of weeks."

The specialist's very words ! He had given the whole bally show away ! But Tom seemed actually reassured by his answer.

After a pause Tom said : " Do you know what he asked me ? Asked me if I had gone with loose women ! " Mansie glanced at him in alarm. " Fancy asking a fellow a thing like that ! " Tom went on. " A funny set, these doctors, I must say ! "

" He had no right to ask you that ! " exclaimed Mansie. It was going a bit too far, and the fellow dying ! " It was a dashed insult ! "

But he was thinking : That was the first thing that Doctor Black had asked too.

Tom looked out through the window : " Oh,

I told him off all right. Still, it was a damned cool thing to ask a chap." The cab was rolling along Sauchiehall Street. " I see they've opened a new cinema there."

" Yes, cinemas going up all over the show now," said Mansie. " Money in them too. Pay as much as 40 per cent., some of them."

But Tom seemed to be profoundly dejected all at once. Hadn't been in a cinema for a long time, poor chap. Would never see the inside of one again. The thought brought the presence of death very near. Mansie glanced at his brother and hastily turned away his eyes again. What could one talk to him about ? A matter of months, perhaps of weeks. This cab was taking a terribly long time. Only Union Street still. If you could only get out and walk : do something !

The dull afternoon brightened ; they were crossing the Jamaica Bridge now. Tom put his head out through the window and sniffed as if he felt the sea air. The rusty funnels of a tramp steamer showed over the low parapet of the bridge. Tom sat with his head just inside the window ; he seemed turned to stone. Then he lay back in his corner with a thud. Thinking of the sea, no doubt, poor beggar. Eglinton Street. These squalling children. You could hear them here all right ; seemed to be right down among them. Orange-peel on the pavement. The red-haired woman, As usual. Everything unchanged. Would this cab never get there?

At last the cab stopped. There was the close, right enough. And Mansie eagerly pushed Tom up the stairs as if he still feared that he would never get him delivered. Mrs. Manson was waiting in the doorway.

"It's all right, mother," said Mansie. "The specialist expects he'll be better in a matter of weeks, but it may be months."

It came quite easy now. Queer how easy a fellow got used to it. Tears started to Mrs. Manson's eyes, and she silently took Tom by the hand. They went in. Delivered safely.

When Tom was settled in his chair by the kitchen fire Jean made a sign to Mansie and left the room. He found her standing by the window in the parlour. "No hope," he said, and he repeated the specialist's words.

"Your mother mustn't be told," was all that Jean said. Then she went back to the kitchen.

Mansie walked through to his room and lay down on the bed. Took it out of a fellow. Wouldn't like to go through that again. Helen. Have to write to her. But he lay where he was without moving. Too dashed tired. He awoke with a start. Why, he must have fallen asleep; it was quite dark. He got up and lit the gas. Have to write that letter. The thought exasperated him. Well, better get it over. But there was no letter-paper in his room. Dash it, what

if there was none in the house! That would be
the bally limit. At last he found a writing-block
in the kitchen, and ignoring his mother's advice
that he should write in comfort at the kitchen
table, bore it back to his room, sat down on the
bed and with a resolute air took out his fountain
pen. But the sight of the letter-block reminded
him of all the letters he had written to Helen,
letters beginning with terms of endearment that
he could never use again, and the strength went
out of his fingers. It couldn't be true that he
would never see her again! That couldn't be
the meaning of this letter that he was going to
write to her! It couldn't be! Tom couldn't be
dying on them like this! Dash it all, were they
doing any harm to anybody? It seemed hard
lines that they had to give each other up because
Tom got a clout on the head falling off a tramcar.
But as though this were merely a rhetorical
protest by a spectator watching an impersonal
process accomplishing itself, his fingers gripped
the pen and wrote the words, " Dear Helen."
Fatal words; for at the sight of them his heart
hardened and he went on setting down one short
sentence after another, as though he were doling
out in minute doses some strange and dreadful
substance – for it did not seem to come out of
him at all: " Tom has seen the specialist to-day.
The specialist says there is no hope. Tom may
live for a few months, or it may be only weeks.

In these circumstances I feel we cannot go on.
It would be better not to see each other again.
I hope you will forgive me and see that this is not
my fault. I think you will agree that we cannot
go on. I trust you will be happy in the future."
He stopped and gazed at the written page. He
felt very tired. Should he add anything more?
What more could he say? He pondered for a
moment and then signed his name. A queer
end to that day on the cliffs outside Gourock!
Oh, dash it, dash it! Must stick to the house and
Tom now. Enough to keep any fellow occupied.

He put on his hat, went out to the corner, and
dropped the letter in the post-box. All the tramcars were packed with people returning from their
work.

PART THREE

22

In the National Gallery in London there is a picture of Christ in the Garden of Gethsemane by Giovanni Bellini. The dawn is wakening and on the high hill to the north the walls of Jerusalem are rosy against a night sky sullenly dissolving away. The garden, a coign of clean and carven rock, a little wave-like shell of stone, lies in a hollow where the shadow is like clear water. In the cup of this shell recline the three disciples in a slumber that looks more like a trance, so rigid are their postures, so blind and rebellious their faces. To the right the basin swells up to a thick frill of rock, where, overlooking the ultimate curved crest of the wave in whose trough the sleepers lie, Christ kneels with arms upraised towards the dark mountains, His face turned away from His followers. He is a powerful, deep-chested man with reddish-fair hair and beard, and one can see that the bars of the cross will take a long time to break Him. In the middle ground, between Jerusalem's hill and Gethsemane, a handful of soldiers are straggling along a country road. The road does not lead

towards Gethsemane but runs at right angles to
it, and one might imagine at first that the soldiers
are making for some other destination, until one
sees that the road presently bends round. Christ's
eyes are lifted to the mountains. Has He seen
the soldiers ? It is impossible to tell ; but if He
should turn His head, it will not be the familiar
fields and roads that He will see, but a stage on
which He can watch, as if it were somebody
else's, the unfolding of His personal fate. And
where the road bends towards Him the soldiers
will become taller and He will see that their eyes
are fixed on Him.

Somewhat like this is the apparently fortuitous
and yet deliberate approach of a disease which
intends to remain for a long time with its object,
and can afford at leisure to fulfil its purposes.
All that the watcher may discern at first is a tiny
moving shape at the head of some remote mountain path. He watches it with an uneasiness
that he cannot explain, for the road forks many
times before it passes his house, and there are
many populated valleys among the mountains
to which it may be going. Presently the path is
hidden behind one of the peaks of that country,
a mountain so high and broad that it blots the
very memory of the traveller from his mind.
But several days later he again remembers and
looks up towards the mountains. Nothing is
moving, the road is bare, and he is about to turn

back and walk into his house, when, far nearer
than he had thought of looking, he sees the
traveller still steadily walking on. His heart
contracts; for although still a long distance
away, the traveller is now in his valley. When,
still at the same deliberate pace, the moving
figure turns up the path that leads to the
watcher's door, the watcher retreats a little
within the threshold as though to hide himself,
and peering out still hopes: Not for me! For
my mother, my wife, my child! But not a word
is spoken when at last the visitor's shadow falls
across the threshold stone; the householder's
body stiffens for a moment, but then he sits down
on a chair and stares at the clear swathe of light
falling uninterruptedly now across the doorway.

Afterwards he has no need to strain his eyes
looking for his visitor, for they are never separated. Yet he still keeps an anxious watch, but
now it is on his wife and mother and child, for
though he still lives in his own house, and has
indeed inscrutably become a prisoner there,
everything has become strangely remote, for his
new companion now bears him away on a spectral
journey in which all that was once familiar to
him recedes to a fabulous distance; and when
his wife Helen or his mother speaks to him, often
he does not answer, for they are so far away that
even if he were to shout his voice would never
reach them; and besides his visitor's silence

so encompasses him that he has grown into it.

At the beginning he manages occasionally to shake off his companion's voiceless converse for a few hours; but the return to it is dreadful. But most dreadful of all is that when he takes off his clothes at night and stretches himself on his bed – from which his wife has been banished, for he has entered on his celibacy – his companion lies down quietly beside him and takes him in his arms. Every morning automatically proffers an instant's hope; awakening he lies looking at the floor, on which a little strip of light is already stretched, and, his mind vacantly clinging to it, he wonders why the hour should be so late and he still in bed; then he remembers, and the hope stealthily emerges: he cautiously puts out his hand and feels the arm around him. He lies for a little staring into the face beside him on the pillow, and then as though in defiance he feels his arms and the arch of his chest, which are still powerful in spite of all that his enemy has done. He savours his defiance for a little; it is a luxury that he has learned he may safely indulge, for such things as these do not move his companion to retaliation; he may even curse, if the inclination takes him, more, he may insultingly ignore his companion altogether. But all this liberty freely allotted him is only a cheat; suddenly he gazes in front of him as though he had remembered something unpleasant, gets up, and puts on his clothes. As he does so he cannot help once more prodding with the tips of his fingers his arms and legs, which still look round and strong; yet now he is not so sure; he has grown fatter; it is as though he had assumed a new casing of fat as a protection against his enemy, had retreated behind a quivering wall of fat; but it is unavailing, a stupid ruse of the dumb body, and he has ceased to believe in the efficacy of the tissue that so warmly laps him round.

When he sits down to breakfast under the anxious eyes of his mother, once more it is an act of defiance to his visitor. He eats greedily, yet it is an unnatural act, for it is only his body that is eating, and he is aware of the chewed balls of food being driven by a deliberately perverse act of the will down into his stomach, there to enrich his blood and secrete fat to plump his skin. For what? And he feels for a moment that he has been treacherously feeding his enemy. His palate is flat and wooden, and he rises from the table with a hollow nausea, as though he had been participating in an unclean rite. Going outside he walks up and down before the house, slowly, for his left leg jerks forward and swings back again in a strange way, drawn by some external force he has never hitherto been very clearly aware of; it is the force of gravity. He looks at the trees and the stony mountains; once they were a source from which he could draw an infinite supply of health; the cool breath of the leafage refreshed him, the hot breath of the burnt rock lulled his senses; but now everything is hard and sterile; the trees are dead wood and even the leaves are sharp; when autumn comes they will be sharp as blades. His eyes seek the pool lying in shadow in the hollow below the house; he would like to sink far down in it, for then he might get relief; yet he can scarcely tell now whether in that thought of relief the thought of death may not have quietly concealed itself. Nevertheless he feels assuaged, looking at the pool; but then his eyes stray again to the unfriendly trees and hills, and he turns and sees his wife and his mother standing at the door. They too are unfriendly now, for they cannot help him; nothing can help him, neither the cool morning, nor the embalmed evening air. He goes in, the women making way for him, and sits down on the hard chair beside the fireless hearth; for the dead wooden arms of the chair on which his hands rest are no more dead than all those trees standing in their thousands with drooping leaves in the heat; they are nothing but wood, nothing but wood to the core.

So his stationary journey conducts him to more and more arid and waterless regions; but in his dreams his progress is sometimes reversed, and the presence he has been so long accustomed to once more advances upon him as though for the first time. But now it advances with rushing speed. He is in a vast city and he is safe for the moment, for he is lying in a small room at the end of a high-walled street so narrow that it scarcely gives room for a man to pass. His sleep is alarmed by a distant sound, the ghostly brazen clank of some vehicle rushing through the streets. It seems to be miles and miles away, in some distant suburb. Where can it be going? What strange load can it be carrying? He hears it boring its labyrinthine way through stony gullies lit by electric moons like clocks all pointing to the same blank hour; he tries to waken himself, for what if it should be coming to him? But he cannot tear his eyelids open, although the dinning now clashes round him like the waves of a brazen sea, sinking and swelling as the house blocks muffle it and set it free again. Then with a glare of lights the tramcar flashes down on him and hits him full on the head; he puts up his hand and screams. At last he opens his eyes; people are standing round his bed; yes, there they all are, his mother and the rest of them. He looks round; everything in the room is where it had been before; everything is quiet; but his companion has laid his hand, gently, on his head: the laying on of hands. And now, while his mother busies herself with wet cloths, he knows that he must set himself to endure a long ordeal. The pressure is gentle still, but gradually

it increases; he sets his teeth, the pain softly
bores in and in, he breaks out into words at
which his mother turns her face away; but it is
of no use, and like a child being whipped he
sobs, begging for relief for this one time: the
pressure tightens. And to a shadow standing in
the dim gaslight he cries: " Shoot me, Mansie,
shoot me ! " But then as though his companion
were only after all tickling him in a particularly
ingenious way, his limbs begin to jerk, his face
grows red with humiliation and agony, the cry
" Oh Christ ! " bursts from him, and his arms
stretch out like rods, his fingers clench the edge
of the bed, the pupils of his open eyes roll round
and round like planets whirled out of their orbits,
and a long and trembling sigh is expelled through
his nostrils, which quiver like those of a snarling
dog; it is as though in that long sigh he were
trying to breathe out the hard ball of pain. In a
little his leaden stupor passes again into sleep.

He awakens next morning shaken and relieved,
for having broken him the pain has left its
habitation. He lies on in comfortable vacancy,
lies longer than usual, and in a half-doze almost
forgets his companion. Towards midday he
rises and still half in a dream walks up and down
before the house. Behind the walls of his dream
the trees and hills have receded, and he realises
that with a leap last night has borne him on for
another great stretch of his invisible journey.

And although his senses are still drugged, and he refuses to emerge from the lulling stupor in which he walks, he cannot keep his heart from turning over; yet that spasm is ineffectual and irrelevant, like the straining of a body under an anæsthetic. When he tries to think now of what he would like most in the world, he discovers that his desires cannot reach back beyond the time of his captivity; if he could but be as he was yesterday he would be happy, and the days when he fearfully scanned the mountain path seem an impossible dream.

At last he reaches a stage in his changing progress where he can tell no longer in which world he is moving, that of humanity clothed in the same vesture as his own, or that of his unearthly companion. When neighbours come to the house he looks at their sunburnt faces with distant eyes and cannot quite conceal his aversion; his glance appraisingly runs over their shoulders, arms and legs, as it might over a horse which he would not buy at any price, knowing that it cannot be depended on. Nor do his eyes change whether it is male or female that is reflected in them; he may stare a little longer than is seemly at the outward spout of the women's breasts, but a sick man has privileges, and although those spheres may bring to his mind, now arid as dried bone, the thought of gushing fountains, their existence seems as mechanical as that of a spring bubbling up and maintaining incessantly its glassy bell-like shape by a perpetual feat of illusion ; and besides he has no longer any desire, parched though he is, to drink of those waters. For now he lives in a world of impersonal forces, a world where anything less than infallibility is insufficient and almost shameful, and where there are only straight lines. He has grown so far beyond the normal human stature which men call maturity, that even those who pride themselves on having put away childish things seem to him children or at best clumsy adolescents. For much as they may talk of necessity not one of them understands the word " must " ; and although they admit perhaps that there is no appeal against and no reprieve from the powers that rule their fates, they are incapable of believing it, for they still hope to escape. And when his mother, perhaps out of over-anxiety, fails to understand some casual sign, he gives her a deadly look ; but it is not lack of love or solicitude that he hates her for ; it is lack of infallibility, for infallibility is the only thing that can save a man beset by infallible forces.

When he sees this, it is the beginning of despair. Yet sometimes he thinks that if he were a clever man he would be content to give all his mind to the foiling of his enemy, content to pass the rest of his life up to old age in that

impersonal and stationary combat; and if in the
midst of the fight he should be snatched away by
some irrelevant accident, a vulgar epidemic or
mere old age, he reflects that he would go
willingly, for that too would be a triumph over
his enemy. For it is no longer death that he is
fighting, but the infallible consummation of an
objective process.

So he has to think impersonally and infallibly,
and not like ordinary people ruled by such blind
motions as love and fear and pity. Yet sometimes it seems to him that this very imperson-
ality which he opposes to his enemy is merely the
last capitulation, the habituation to the inevitable.
Then in terror he seeks an escape, he flies back
to fallible human contacts, and with lowered eyes,
ashamed and threatening, dreams of admission
to his wife's bed. But it is a sad and unnatural
physiological experiment, a trivial post-mortem
ecstasy in an automatic hell where only the flesh
still lives. Afterwards he may lie by his wife's
side while the tears flow down his cheeks, but
then with averted face he finds himself in his
own bed, where he remains in a despair so
profound that he does not even notice his companion lying beside him.

In this final redoubt of despair, beleaguered by
forces which are neither cruel nor benevolent,
but merely pitiless, at the very last moment he
appeals to a power beyond them, a power as

infinitely loving as they are infinitely without love.
And although hitherto he has clearly recognised
his sufferings as a dispensation from God, now
he appeals to God from them and sees no con-
tradiction in his appeal.   Yet – for he has learnt
cunning – he does it stealthily, so stealthily that,
in spite of his wild desire that God should hear
and answer him, he leaves a last hope : the hope
that God may not have heard.   For if God
were to hear and yet not answer, his faith might
perish, and dying he might despair even of death.
At last, when no answer comes, the hour of
resignation breaks in gently and brutally, des-
troying everything but itself ; and he is resigned
to all, to God, to his persecution, to his agony, to
the fabulous waterless regions through which he
is now more and more dizzily whirled, and to the
thought of the death of his body.

        This last stage is so hateful to human eyes that
even the involuntary object of the metamorphosis can hardly be contemplated without a
faint but deep feeling of aversion.   Those who
are nearest him have now perpetually the look
that can be seen in the eyes of people returning
to their house after saying good-bye to a son or a
brother who has set out on a journey from which
it is unlikely that he will ever return ; it is a look
in which despair, resignation and a trace of relief
are mingled.   And although he has not actually
gone away, but still lies there in the bed, they

take no pains to conceal this look; they gaze
upon him, tenderly but with a little aversion, as
on something whose presence is inexplicably
troubling, with those eyes that have already said
farewell. This aversion lasts until the final
moment of metamorphosis. But then hatred
both of death and his victim falls away, and in
astonishment the living see that something
stranger than they could ever have imagined has
been accomplished. And looking at the face, so
remote now that even the white sheet that touches
it seems to have far more of the pathetic associa-
tions of mortality, they are wafted on to a shore
so strange that they can find no name for it;
they stand on the very edge of Time, they stand
there as in a sleep, and dread lest they might
awaken and Time be no longer there with them.

23

IN A HOUSE of sickness, as in any house, the ordinary routine of the day must be observed. The breadwinner must get up in the morning and go to work ; the meals must be on the table at the appointed hours ; fires have to be kindled, floors swept, beds made, brass scoured, dishes washed and dried. Yet all those daily offices whose very monotony once gave a sense of comfort, as though they were a perpetually renewed covenant securing the day's peace and order, become meaningless once the covenant has been repudiated by the other invisible party to it, and is left in one's hands, a useless piece of paper whose terms nevertheless bind one, strangely enough, as absolutely as before. So even the simplest household tasks which Mrs. Manson had performed with automatic ease for many decades would on some days rise up before her as alarming problems that she needed all her skill to solve, and she would look round the kitchen as if everything in it – the range, the brass taps, the pots and pans – had grown strange and hostile ; and it was a mathematical labour to

move the table from the wall to the middle of the
floor, and to remember the number of dishes, of
knives and forks and spoons, she had to lay out
on it.   Even when, shortly after Tom's visit to
the specialist, Jean threw up her job and took over
most of the housework, Mrs. Manson was still
dazed by the little that remained for her ; the
routine of the house had become a piece of recal-
citrant machinery whose workings she had pain-
fully to foresee and provide against, and it in-
spired her with something of the dread that she
felt for all machinery : for the tramcars rushing
about the streets, for the cash tickets neatly shot
out like little sneering tongues by the automatic
cash registers in the shops, for the dreadful maze
of machinery through which, since he came to
Glasgow, Tom had walked for a time miracu-
lously unscathed, until at last it struck him down.
Often she would stop in the middle of the morning's work and say : " Oh, why did we ever come
here, Jeannie ? "   But she had asked the question so often that she never waited for a reply,
but simply resumed her work again.

Tom became more and more incapable of con-
trolling his limbs, and a few weeks after his visit
to the specialist he had a severe stroke and next
day collapsed on the floor when he was getting
out of bed.   As they lifted him up he said something, but his speech was indistinct – it was as
though his tongue were swollen – and Jean and

Mrs. Manson could not make out his mumbled
words. This made him very angry; he gave
them a furious look and refused to repeat what
he had said. For some time he lay in silence. At
last he said, very slowly and deliberately : " Give
– me – a – drink – of – water," as though he were
repeating a difficult exercise, and when Jean
hastily ran and filled a glass at the tap he looked
at her reproachfully, for her quickness was a
wanton exposure of his new infirmity. So now
he must lie in bed and have everything done for
him.

After this even Mansie gave up hope. Yet a
few days later he wanted to call in another
specialist, and his mother and Jean had to plead
with him for a long time before he gave up the
idea. Surely there was something that could be
done ! It was terrible to sit there with idle hands
and resign yourself to the whole business like his
mother and Jean. But it may have been that he
simply needed to spend to the last penny the
money that still lay in the bank for his marriage
with Helen. And possibly the very fact that the
sacrifice was quite useless, that he took no risk
whatever in throwing away all his money on
Tom, made him all the more eager to do it : it
was a sacrifice without even an object to qualify
it, an absolute act uncontaminated by conse-
quences. In any case he was fantastically generous
during those last few weeks, supported the whole

household uncomplainingly on his shoulders, gave his mother every Saturday a far larger allowance than she needed or could use, and was offended when she chid him for his extravagance. It was dashed hard lines for a fellow to be taken to task for trying to do his best for his brother ! But it was for another sacrifice that his mother and Jean felt most genuinely grateful. Mansie did what he had never done before ; he stayed in the house evening after evening. He had grown thin, and his mother sometimes actually pushed him out through the door and made him go for a walk.

At the beginning of an illness, when the presence of the sick man in the house is merely a disagreeable fact, one flies for relief to society which offers the most complete distraction, to people who do not even know that one's brother is ill ; and one is grateful that such society should exist and that one has so many and such diverse friends. But when the illness takes the last turn and enters the short dark high lane that narrows steadily to the final point, to nothing at all, the household of the dying are gradually stripped to the skin, to the bone, are stripped of feeling after feeling, of friend after friend, until nothing and nobody is left except the thoughts and the friends that still come to bear them company, that consent to sit here with them in this oppressive prison half-light between the narrowing

walls, and voluntarily cut themselves off from
life. And any friend who makes that sacrifice is
a visitor from a higher sphere, for a household of
the dying are like a band of outlaws. Society
has turned away from them in its irresistible
onward course, and if one has put one's faith in
society and dreamt of its end when all men will
be happy and beautiful and without pain, one feels
cast off by the universal process itself, a stone
unworthy of the builder of the world, a pariah
like the noseless beggar selling matches on the
bridge. And when your friend talks of the world
outside, he seems to be telling you of things
which no longer concern you, of a country you
have left where great things are being done in
which you can have no part. And in your home-
sickness for it there is the bitterness of the
rejected.

It was now that Bob Ryrie showed his true
mettle. Every evening he dropped in, if only for
a few minutes, to sit and talk by Tom's bed. He
faithfully reported the football match on Saturday, and every evening had some new funny
story to tell. And he seemed to know exactly
what to say to Mrs. Manson as well. Even Jean's
manner changed towards him, and one evening
when Mansie was putting on his hat in the lobby
he heard her saying in the kitchen, in reply to
Mrs. Manson's customary eulogy of their visitor :
" Bob ? Yes, he's a trump." That was high

praise for Jean, and next evening Mansie told Bob
about it.   But although Bob was obviously
pleased, he remained quite cool, accepted the
compliment, one might almost say, as his due.
Well, Jean hadn't treated the fellow very well,
but all the same he might have shown more
appreciation.

Still, Mansie was very proud of Bob. But it
wasn't so easy to explain why Brand should have
begun to come about the house again. Nobody
wanted him in any case ; even Jean didn't seem
particularly pleased to see him.   After staying
away all the summer when Tom was able to
move about and talk like a human being, it was
almost indecent of him to come to the house
now when Tom was pinned to his bed and
unable even to protest.   And it wasn't as if he
came to see Tom ; didn't care a hang, seemingly,
how the poor chap was.   Besides one couldn't
take him in to see Tom ; Tom couldn't stand the
fellow ; and so one had to sit with him in the
parlour and talk about the I.L.P. and Guild
Socialism – his latest fad, what would the
weathercock take up next ?   Almost seemed as
if he wanted Tom out of the way before he came
to the house again.   Still, he appeared to be put
out about something or other ; always telling
one to go for walks and look after one's health.
What was that that he had brought out the other
evening ?   Some quotation from Ruskin : that

you should help those that could be helped, not those that were past help. Him and his quotations. Well, if Jean married the fellow she had less sense than he gave her credit for.

But Brand still continued to visit the house and to ask with anxious looks after Mansie's health.

24

A YOUNG man whose heaven has recently altered its position, shooting down from the transcendental to the historical plane, is likely to be thrown into greater bewilderment even than other human beings by the fact of death. For until a year ago death and heaven have been so close to each other in his mind that only an unimaginable something, infinite yet infinitesimal, divided them ; but now they are separated by an immovable expanse of quite ordinary time, by days, weeks and years just like other days, weeks and years, and there remains nothing to connect death which is here with heaven which is merely somewhere else. The secular transplantation of heaven, which should have brought it closer, has removed it to an inaccessible distance, so that not even man's last desperate resort, not even death, is of any avail. And as your mind, no matter how ignorantly, demands a meaning for everything, even for death, you may feel at times that your brother is doing something quite unnatural in dying now, and that, to have any meaning, the act should at least be postponed –

say for a few hundred years : postponed until he
has first known what life can be. It is as though
he were dying in a provisional chaos where
neither life nor death has yet completely evolved
– scarcely even dying therefore, but simply falling into a bottomless hole that swallows everything and gives no sign. And if you suspect in
your heart – even though it is palpably untrue –
that you have robbed your brother of his girl,
you may feel now that you have cheated him of his
legitimate death as well, and substituted for it
something small and commonplace without his
knowing what has happened.

If Mansie Manson felt this, he was hardly aware
of it, for his most articulate sensation was one of
painful and embarrassed repugnance, a repugnance that muffled without softening the icy and
majestic dread which heralds the approach of
death. And that he should feel this embarrassed
repugnance was inevitable, although he did not
know it ; for the new creed he had embraced was
different from all the older faiths of mankind in
one startling respect : that it did not take death
into account at all, but left it as an arbitrary fact,
a private concern of the dead. It took death so
little into account that it could comfortably
transform death into a mere moment in the progress of life towards its Utopian goal, a necessary
and indeed progressive factor in human destiny ;
for how except through death could the

ever-advancing armies of the generations relieve
one another ? It socialised death so radically as to
forget altogether that it is human beings who die,
and that all human beings must die. It transmuted death into another kind of life, so that,
pitifully isolated in your ego and in time, you
could still believe that you would live on in the
lives, as pitifully isolated, of the legatees of your
breath; or that, consigned to the earth, you
would enjoy at least a sort of immortality in
the fortuitous flowers that might spring from
your dust, a chemical or biochemical immortality through which finally, it might be,
you would enter in some appropriate incarna-
tion into the chemical bliss of your far distant
Utopia.

Not having any great intelligence or sincerity
of mind Mansie Manson was quite incapable of
perceiving this; as incapable as he was of seeing
that, in spite of its extreme Utopianism, his faith
contained as necessarily as the strictest Calvinism
a dogma of reprobation. A dogma of reprobation far more sweeping, indeed, than Calvin's,
for until the gates of the earthly heaven are
opened all who die are automatically lost. Automatically, for it does not matter whether you
have striven for that heaven or perversely turned
your back upon it; in either case you are lost
" by a just and irreprehensible, but incompre-
hensible, judgment " : Calvin's words used in

another connection apply with just as over-whelming cogency to you.

All this Mansie might have discovered had he chosen, or been able, to understand the Marxian interpretation of history, which for all its harsh-ness is the true theology of every Utopian reli-gion. But he was quite incapable of understand-ing it, or of seeing that the penalty for certainty in any faith, heavenly or earthly, is some form of predestination, involving election and damna-tion. He accepted the inevitability of the heaven with which Marx's economic doctrine had pre-sented him, but he disliked Marxians as heartily as a popular religious enthusiast dislikes theolo-gians who insist on demonstrating the necessity of hell. They were a set of sordid-minded materialists who kept nice people out of the movement.

Yet now that Tom lay on his back unable to stir or to speak, passively submitting to the automatic process of death, Mansie, while still clinging to his far distant heaven, felt that Tom was incomprehensibly and irretrievably lost, lost as one might be who had died on a world frozen to rigidity long before this world came into existence. Heaven still floated before him at just the same point in the future ; it had not changed its position by a hand's breadth ; but it was as though he realised for the first time exactly how far away it was.

And then, in a clap, the feelings that he had had
on the Sunday when he walked to Strathblane,
and many times in his childhood, returned again.
He felt as he had done when a boy, looking at
the farm planted precariously on the side of the
hill, that the position of his heaven was in some
inexplicable way wrong, so deeply wrong that it
filled him with apprehension. He felt that it was
not where it should be ; yet when he dreamt of
another station for it he became blind and could
see nothing but a shining vacancy. It was a
vague sense of ill-ease that he felt, and it never
hardened into a definite thought. But had he
been able to read his mind he would have found,
strangely enough, that what he longed for was
not to bring his dreamt-of heaven nearer, so near
that he would be able to see it outspread before
him and cross its frontiers and be received finally
within it, stepping out of a dying world into one
new born, but rather to raise his heaven to some
position high above itself, to lever it upwards
with his eyebeams to a height where it would no
longer be in Time ; for so long as it was in Time,
Time would sunder him from it. And with his
sense of separation his old dread of chaos returned, for chaos is universal separation ; and
at the uttermost end of the blind longing to lift
his heaven from the distant future place where it
stood so implacably, there must have been the
hope that if it could be raised high enough,

uplifted to an inconceivable height, Time would once more become whole and perfect, and a meaning be given not only to present death, but to all the countless dead lying under their green mounds, so that the living and the dead and the unborn might no longer be separated by Time, but gathered together in Time by an everlasting compact beyond Time. All that he felt was an uneasy sense that even the perfect future state was not all that it should be ; but when, brooding on Tom's certain death, he said as he often did now, " Well, there's no use in expecting a miracle to happen," he was probably thinking, without knowing it, of a greater miracle. But he had no hope that it would happen.

25

Bob Ryrie had finished his account of the afternoon's football. He got up and said : " Well, so long, Tom, see you again to-morrow." In the lobby he turned to Mansie : " Can I speak to you for a minute ? " and he pushed open the parlour door. Mansie followed him and lit the gas. The venetian blinds were not down, and the blank window looked like a hole let into the room, leaving it perilously exposed.

Bob cleared his throat. But after all he did not speak for quite a while. At last he said : " Helen's been to see me." It was the first time that Helen's name had been mentioned between them since Mansie had announced the breaking of the engagement.

Mansie stared at the floor. He was standing beneath the chandelier and the light falling on his head again made him feel exposed. She's gone to him next, he thought. Hasn't wasted much time. She'll never be at a loss for anyone to take her part, by gum ! " Well ? " he said.

" Mansie," said Bob, " is it all off between

you ? " He added hastily : " Helen's been going
through a pretty rotten time, you know."

" It's all off," said Mansie. " And I can't
discuss it." The exposed window troubled
him ; Bob and he seemed to be standing there
as on a stage. Almost like rivals.

" All right, Mansie, all right. I don't want to
interfere. But I thought you would like to
know—— Well, we won't say any more about
it."

They stood in silence for a few moments ;
but the window still troubled Mansie, and as if
confronting a danger, he walked over to it.
There, looking out into the foggy darkness with
his back to Bob, he said : " Bob, do you think
I'm to blame in this business ? "

Bob cleared his throat again : " This business ?
You mean Helen ? "

" No," Mansie jerked out, swinging his arm
towards the kitchen, " Tom."

" Come, come, you're overwrought, Mansie.
You're getting fancies into your head. I can say
this, and I defy anybody to deny it : you've done
everything a brother could have done for Tom."

" Yes, yes, I know," said Mansie, still looking
out through the window. Then he burst out :
" If it hadn't been for my going with that girl
this might never have happened ! I wish to God
I had never set eyes on her, Bob ! "

Bob was silent again. At last he began in an

embarrassed voice : " I don't see——" Then,
as if taking a plunge : " She broke with Tom long
before that, you know. She would never have
gone back to him, whatever happened. And
besides – I don't like to say it now – but it was
Tom's own fault. She was actually afraid of
him ; she told me so herself. If Tom had any
grudge against you, it was all pure imagination.
And he knows it now. And besides Tom was
always a little too fond of a glass ; you know
that as well as I do. He might have tumbled off
a car on his head any time these last two years.
It was sheer good luck he didn't do it before."

Mansie listened vigilantly. Bob was certainly
pretty cool about the business ! He said : "Well,
it may be." Then he burst out : " But a fellow
would like to be sure ! "

" Mansie, you never did anything intentionally
against Tom. Keep that fixed in your mind.
It's only his intentional actions that any fellow
can be held responsible for. You shouldn't stick
to the house so much, you know. Makes you
begin to fancy things. Well, I must be going."
Bob looked at his watch. " I'm late. I'll have
to hurry."

Mansie escorted him to the door. Earlier in
the evening he had had thoughts of taking a turn
with Bob himself, but Bob was evidently in a
great hurry to meet someone else. Who could it
be ? A girl ? And suddenly Mansie knew : it

was Helen. He glanced into Bob's face. " Well,
good luck, Bob," he said, and he could not
refrain from adding bitterly, " I hope you have a
pleasant evening."

" Right ! " said Bob hastily. " Right ! So
long, Mansie." And he turned and literally flew
downstairs.

Mansie returned to the parlour. So Bob was
off for a pleasant evening. Kissing and cuddling.
First Tom, then me, then Bob. She should be
satisfied now, by gum. Made you want to spit.
But it was downright indecent to go straight
off to Bob, to one's best friend. Was she to make
trouble between all the fellows she could get her
claws into ? By gum, she wouldn't do it this
time, she wouldn't make trouble between him
and Bob ; he would see to that. Though Bob
might have shown a little more delicacy. It
wasn't like him. But that woman had got round
him, and she was equal to anything. Kissing and
cuddling and Tom dying. And she couldn't
even have forgotten the feel of Tom's kisses yet!
Well, he was glad he had cleared out. Hard
lines on Bob, in a way ; almost as if he had been
let in for it ; but he dashed well deserved all he
got, behaving like that !

Mansie went on walking to and fro between the
window and the door. The fog outside had
grown thicker. He let down the blinds. Kissing
and cuddling. A fellow couldn't stay here

evening after evening ! Must go out once in a
while ; Saturday night too ; all Glasgow out
enjoying itself and him chained here. Might try
a music-hall, the Pavilion or the Alhambra, and
be among people and see and hear something
cheerful for a change. Kissing and cuddling.
A fellow couldn't go on like this ! A fine life !
He went through to the kitchen. His mother
and Jean, sitting before the fire, looked up ;
Tom seemed to be asleep.

" I think I'll go out for a little, mother," he
said, " if you can spare me."

" Do that, my lamb, you need a change."

But when he was sitting on the top of the
crowded tramcar suddenly he felt discour-
aged. All the seats would be booked up ; no
hope of getting one at that hour ; what was the
use of trailing from one music-hall to another ?
So he got off at Gordon Street and wandered into
the Central Station. But nobody was there ;
the book- and tobacco-stalls were closed, and
the electric lights hung blankly high up in the fog
under the roof ; the place looked as if it hadn't
been used for years. He walked out into Union
Street. Although the station was deserted the
pavement here was packed from side to side with
a moving mass of people, and looking down from
the steps he saw bowler hats and upturned faces
on which the electric lamps shed a fitful glare,
coating cheek-bones and eye-sockets as with a

luminous and corrosive oil. The pavement, though completely filled, gave passage-way for two sluggish processions that moved in opposite directions, and from where he stood these two processions seemed to be standing each on a long raft that moved with them at a steady speed to some destination that could not be imagined, bore them away without paying any regard to their wishes; for some of them had the air of unwilling captives, while others seemed impatient at the slowness with which they were carried forward. Yet though their progress was so inexorable, it left time for a group of young men here and there to shout inviting or lewd words to the girls on the other raft as it floated past, words that evoked stony stares or tittering or raucous laughter. But at the same time these two rafts bearing all that human freightage floated just a little above the mud, were only a thin partition over a bottomless quagmire, and through the planks the mud oozed up and clung to the passengers' shoe-soles, though their heads were so high in the air. If the whole business were to collapse! Mansie pushed his way through the moving mass and stepped on to the roadway. Safer there, though it was damp and sticky, like Eglinton Street. There was no help for it; one had just to walk right round a crowd like that. Swaggering there under the electric lights and shouting filth at each other. And people dying!

He came to the corner of St. Vincent Street.
The street lay before him completely dark and
silent, a blank wall of fog, and he plunged into
it as though a thin paper wall hiding oblivion
or nonentity. But the zone in which he found
himself was not completely blank, as might have
been thought; for as he walked on there went
with him a small intimate circular area of clarity,
a private area in which he was far more alone
than he could ever have been in a room. And
with a shiver of fear he knew that he could no
longer escape, here in this perambulating privacy,
from the thought that had been trying to catch
him all evening. Was he to blame for Tom's
death? Oh God, could he be to blame? He
turned a corner as if to escape from the question.
Where could he be now? Tram-lines. Must be
West Nile Street. Hard if a fellow was to be
held responsible for a thing he never intended!
Never even in his thoughts! Was it his fault
that Tom took a glass too much that night and
stumbled as he got off the tramcar? What had
he to do with that? How could he have helped
it? (Dangerous things these cars; must be
careful.) And was it just that Tom should have
to die of a tumour on the brain simply because
of that one clout on the head? Seemed a pretty
heavy punishment for taking one glass too much.
And maybe it wasn't Tom's fault at all! The car
driver may have had too much drink himself and

stopped the car with a jerk ; that often happened. And was that Tom's fault ? It was the car driver's, if it was anybody's. And Tom had to die for it after all these months with that pain in his head. And just after the fellow had turned over a new leaf too. Seemed dashed unjust.

Mansie turned another corner and passed a church. Its grimy walls had the look of many city churches ; as though they had been defiled by innumerable passing dogs, or by a long succession of drunken men overcome by need and pathetically willing to find any wall a urinal. That church in Eglinton Street. Those hooligans were still standing there, no doubt. As cocky as ever. Nothing happened to *them*. *They* were allowed to do what they dashed well liked seemingly. By gum, they would know how to treat a tart like Helen, all the same. For that was what she was, in spite of her refined airs. Tom was quite right in calling her what he did that evening. And now she was walking with Bob. In the fog where nobody could see them. Safe and cosy. Took dashed good care that nothing ever happened to *her*. *She* never went through Eglinton Street. It was simple fellows like Tom that had to pay the penalty. The menacing thought came nearer. He quickened his pace. Women ! They always knew how to go scot-free. No, he wasn't to blame ! He was dashed if he was to blame.

He came to an open space. Tall shapes rose round him in the fog. George Square. High up, the electric lamps flung down cones of bluish light on the stony heads and shoulders of the smoke-grimed statues. It was dashed uncanny, all these figures standing there without moving. Standing there for ever so long, some of them for a hundred years maybe. Must seem a queer world to them if they were to waken up now, frighten them out of their wits, think they were in the next world. That tall one was Burns, couldn't even see his head. No electric light in his time, maybe no fog either. The banks o' Doon. I'll steal awa' to Nannie. And then this. The world was a terrible place, when you came to think of it. Burns had some dashed bad hours in his lifetime. All these women he got in the family way. But none so bad as he would have if he were to waken up here now. Like johnnies frozen stiff and cold ; the last fellows left on the earth might look like this. Would the earth be covered with fog then ? Scooting through space, dead, the whole dashed lot of them, frozen stiff in the fog. Nobody left to care a hang for the poor beggars.

An immense pity for all those figures staring into the fog, left stranded there in the fog, came over him, and he felt a longing to see human faces again, even if it were only those people parading Union Street.

But when he reached Union Street again and saw the two solid streams of human beings still mechanically flowing, apparently quite unchanged, although now different bowler hats, different cheek-bones and eye-sockets were borne on the dim surface under the misty electric lights, he took the first tramcar that came as though it were an ark riding an advancing deluge about to engulf him. And as he sat on the top of the lighted tramcar he felt somewhat as if he were in an ark, felt almost grateful to the other passengers for allowing him to join them, for picking him from the jaws of danger and taking him into this company of decent fellows. Yet he did not speak to the man sitting beside him, for all those up here in this lighted, enclosed, moving chamber were united by a strangely intimate consciousness of one another, and all at once the knowledge came to him : They have all gone through it. And he was filled with pity for them, a pity quite without patronage, for he himself was included objectively in it. Yes, they had all gone through it. A great weight rolled from his heart.

26

JEAN and Mrs. Manson were changing Tom's bed and body linen.

" Oh, his poor, poor ribs ! It breaks your heart to see them sticking out o' his skin like that, Jeannie."

" Hush, mother, he feels no pain now."

" Oh, why does he sigh like that ? It's terrible to listen to him sighing and sighing as if something was broken inside him and he couldna' stop. His poor, poor legs. There's no' much flesh on him noo, Jeannie."

" He's at rest now, mother. It's like a sleep."

" How white his skin is. He had aye a fine white skin. Ever since he was a bairn."

" You must think of us now, mother. You still have Mansie and me. Mansie has been a good brother."

" He could lift me up wi' one arm once, and noo I can almost lift him mysel'. Do you mind yon evening when he lifted me up on his shoulder and wadna' let me doon again ? I was frightened oot o' my wits yon night, Jeannie, I can tell

you. He was aye so fu' o' fun. Oh, Tom,
Tom!"

"There, it's finished, mother. He's comfortable now. Sit down by the fire and rest."

27

DINNER was over. Jean was still softly busied with her housework, which gradually, however, seemed to be coming to a standstill, and then everything would be at rest; for after her long battle Mrs. Manson was lying in her room almost as motionless as Tom outstretched to his full length in his coffin; they were both lying there with only a wall between them. Mansie sat by the kitchen fire; he felt relaxed and drowsy; everything was settled, all the funeral arrangements were made. And as the definitive accomplishment of any long and laborious task, even if it be a death, automatically produces a feeling of satisfaction, the satisfaction of something completed, Mansie could not keep a little content from mingling tormentingly with his other feelings. He found relief for it, he almost seemed to escape responsibility for it, in the thought: "Well, Tom is better out of this." But that was not exactly what he meant, nor did the reflection that his mother was relieved now from the long strain quite seem to absolve him; queer thoughts a fellow had, thoughts that didn't seem right when one's dead brother was lying in the house. And under his drowsy relaxation uneasiness began to stir. He glanced across at Jean. What was she thinking? Was she thinking the same thing? An overpowering longing seized him to look in Tom's face again, to reassure himself finally, to see once and for all, even if at what he saw a fear should start up that he would never forget all his life. And he furtively glanced at Jean, to see that she was still intent and busy, before he left the room.

At the parlour door he waited for a little, then softly turned the handle. The sharp scent of lilies met him, and darkness, for the venetian blinds were down. He stood in the doorway breathing in the scent of the lilies, in which the sharpness of death itself seemed concentrated, and it froze him, so that it was with icy fingers, fingers so numb that they did not feel like his own, that he mechanically closed the door and opened the slats of the venetian blinds, letting in the dull December light. He turned and walked back to the door again before he dared to lift his eyes to the place where the coffin stood; he must have a way of retreat behind him. Then, exerting all his strength, he lifted his eyes.

The light was dim, but Tom was there, almost within reach of his hand. He saw the face with startling vividness, more clearly, it seemed to him, than he had ever seen it before; and as if death had restored Tom to himself, tranquilly reinstating him anew in his body, which had been usurped those many months by a mad and suffering pretender, Mansie realised, as if for the first time, that this was his young brother. How handsome and fine-looking he was! How serious and distant and proud! So this was his brother. Mansie gazed at the face opened to him in death, and all the things that he had been unable or too dulled by custom to read in it while Tom wore it as one living identification mask among many others, a useful everyday mask announcing that here was a fellow called Tom Manson – all these qualities, now absolutely simplified in death, and in that process themselves become absolute and pure, were written clearly on his face, and Mansie saw that his brother had been strong and generous and brave. No, he had never known Tom, never known that he was like this though they had grown up together and lived in the same house. But indeed Tom looked changed, he looked younger, as though in putting off life he had put off at the same time all that had thwarted and defaced it, all that had clouded the lofty fate for which, his brow declared so clearly now, he had been born.

Mansie stood without moving, breathed in the scent of the lilies, and no longer felt any desire to go away; for though he knew that he was standing here in the parlour with his dead brother,

something so strange had happened that it would
have rooted him to a place where he desired far
less to be : the walls had receded, the walls of the
whole world had receded, and soundlessly a vast
and perfect circle – not the provisional circle of
life, which can never be fully described – had
closed, and he stood within it. He did not know
what it was that he divined and bowed down
before: everlasting and perfect order, the eternal
destiny of all men, the immortality of his own
soul ; he could not have given utterance to it,
although it was so clear and certain ; but he had
a longing to fall on his knees. It was not death
that he knelt before ; he did not know indeed to
what he was kneeling, or even whether he was
kneeling ; for his head might have been bowed
by the weight of immortality, by the crushing
thought of that eternal and perfect order in which
he had a part. He did not go down on his knees ;
perhaps a sense of shame restrained him ; he
stood with his eyes fixed on Tom's face, though
now he scarcely saw it, and everything seemed
clear to him : he saw his long struggle to justify
himself towards Tom as a perverse and obstinate
and yet quite simple error, inconceivable in front
of this greatness ; he understood why he had
felt, after the May Day procession, that his happiness had been made of the wrong substance ;
for nothing less than death could erase all wrong
and all memory of wrong, leaving the soul free

for perfect friendship : and, his heart pierced, he
knew that Tom could never have completely
forgiven him but for this, no, never but for this.
Never while they both lived could he and Tom
have found that perfect friendship for which
every human being longed ; for even if Tom had
freely forgiven him, memory, which only died
with the body, would have remained between
them. No, never on earth could that dream be
realised ; he saw this with perfect clearness ;
yet now he was no longer ashamed of his feelings
on May Day, though in the twinkling of an eye
they had become as pathetic as the make-believe
of children trying to penetrate, in all reverence,
though quite aware of the deception, into mys-
teries beyond their understanding. But this was
only a dim intuition which he was incapable of
grasping, and all that he felt was that he was
glad he had been there with the others.

Again the longing to kneel down came over
him, imperiously bowing his head, so that now
he looked at the carpet, pensively absorbed
as one might be in the presence of an old
friend whom one can treat like oneself ; and
as if in the stillness of the house all the walls had
fallen, he saw Jean sitting in the kitchen by the
fire, and his mother lying in her room under the
gaslight, and they all seemed to be together in
one place, he and Jean and his mother, united in
boundless gentleness and love, like a family in

the Bible. Bob should be there too, and Brand should come, and Helen should come. And at the thought of all the people who should gather to the house, as in the evening all the exiled workers are gathered to their homes and to themselves, he felt embedded in life, fold on fold; he longed to go at once and look at Jean, as if she herself were life, sitting there by the fire; he wanted to experience again, like someone learning a lesson, all that he had already experienced; for it seemed a debt due by him to life from which he had turned away, which he had walked round until his new road seemed the natural one, although it had led him to places where all life was frozen to rigidity, and the dead stood about in the mist like the statues in George Square. He was in haste to begin, and with a last glance at Tom's face, which he could only dimly discern now, for darkness was falling, he left the room and closed the door after him.